WICKED OMENS

PATRICIA D. EDDY

If you love sexy romantic suspense, I'd love to send you a short story set in Dublin, Ireland. Castles & Kings isn't available anywhere except for readers who sign up for my mailing list! Sign up for my newsletter on my website and tell me where to send your free book!
http://patriciadeddy.com.

CHAPTER ONE

KILLIAN

Power burst from his hands, turning his fingertips black and rather...crispy. Stalking over to his freezer, he grabbed one of his many ice packs. The sizzle as ice met skin made him cringe.

"If *anyone* in this world still made wands..." His familiar, a small black kitten appropriately named Tiny, yawned and started cleaning her paw.

"Shut it, cat."

"If I *were* a cat, perhaps I would 'shut it.' As I am not, go fuck yourself, Killian. You are a terrible witch, and hopelessly incompetent." With her tail in the air, Tiny pranced away, heading for a patch of sunlight in the front window.

"You're supposed to be helping me with this shite. Or have you forgotten the role of a familiar?"

From the other room, Tiny called, "Start acting like a witch and maybe I'll start acting like a familiar."

Killian sank down at the kitchen table, the ice pack

numbing his fingers as he ached for something to dull the pain of failure deep inside him. Every bloody day he tried, and every day, he either injured himself, set fire to something, or—on the worst days—set off a small explosion in the woods behind his property.

The knock at the door startled him, and the ice pack landed on the kitchen tile with a dull *thunk*.

Not now.

But whoever wanted to see him wasn't taking no for an answer. Or even waiting for him to reach the front room. The lock flipped open and the door creaked as sharp footsteps rapped across his hardwood floors. Killian's fingers closed over the silver and iron cuff he'd left on the counter, and he barely managed to snap it around his wrist before Beatrix Pearce, head of the London Coven entered the room.

"Torturing yourself again, Killian?" She tutted softly as she narrowed her ice blue eyes at the cuff and his blackened fingers. With a few whispered words, Beatrix draped her hands over his, and the burning pain faded almost instantly as his skin mended.

Stepping back, she tucked a long strand of white hair back into her bun. "Better?"

"Yes, High Priestess. Thank you," Killian said. He stopped himself before he asked her what she was doing way out here in the Tonbridge countryside. It had been years since Killian had been willing to live in a city—among people. Not since he'd lost control and killed the vampire he'd been falling in love with.

"Your thoughts betray you, witch," Beatrix said. "Perhaps, since I came all this way, you could offer me some tea? Or...something stronger?"

He hated that word. Witch. He'd begged Beatrix more than once to call him a warlock, but Beatrix insisted that was not the proper term and she would not be using it. Trudging to his stove, he lit the burner and added water to the kettle. "To what do I owe this pleasure, High Priestess?"

"You'd best control your tone, young man. You may be one of the most powerful witches of an age, but I can still give you a thrashing." Beatrix examined her nails as Killian opened a tin of black tea and withdrew two bags.

The act of preparing the tea centered him a bit, and by the time he brought the mugs and the sugar bowl he knew Beatrix would want to the table, his emotions were almost under control. At the last moment, he snagged a bottle of bourbon and set it in front of her as well. "My apologies. It has not been an easy day. But that is no excuse for my rudeness."

"No, it is not." Beatrix added two spoonfuls of sugar to her tea along with a healthy pour of bourbon, stirred daintily, and then sighed. "You know of the Witches' Ball and coven meeting in America?"

"Of course. I'm not that much of a fuck-up, High Priestess."

She snorted, then touched her bun again, making sure every hair was in place. "We are not at the coven house. You may call me Beatrix. A one-time dispensation only."

This couldn't be good. Beatrix was well over seventy years old, and some of the other coven members believed her to be closer to *two hundred* and seventy. She did not bend the rules, did not take to casual conversation. She also did not make house calls. She summoned.

After a sip of the steaming liquid, she set the mug down and withdrew an envelope from the pocket of her skirt. "It is a great honor to receive an invitation. I have attended a dozen times. But this year, the letter that arrived was not addressed to me."

Killian choked on his tea as she slid the thick, cream-colored envelope across the table. "Are you having a laugh? No one would invite me. Not unless they had a death wish."

But there on the front, in thick, gold embossing, was his name. Killian Wade, Witch.

Of course they'd include *that word.*

"You should open it," Beatrix said. "Ignoring such a summons can be unwise."

Killian pushed his chair back and stood. "No. I won't touch it."

Her chuckle contained no mirth. "That will end badly for you, Killian."

"Being among other witches will end badly for me, *Beatrix.* Or have you forgotten what I did?" Killian could still hear the screams in his nightmares. Shadows flickered in the corners of the room, and the cuff around his wrist burned his skin as his magic fought to escape.

His memories haunted him. Oliver screaming, burning, dying. Blood dripping from numerous wounds, half his head bashed in, and missing his right hand.

Killian couldn't breathe. He had to get outside. Somewhere he couldn't hurt anyone. Pushing through the back door, he sucked in deep lungfuls of the cool autumn air, staring out over the misty landscape.

"I would not leave that envelope untended for long," Tiny said as she padded lightly into the tall grasses off his back porch. "The New Orleans coven's magic is legendary, and they do not take kindly to being made to wait. If the cottage is destroyed, you are *not* putting me in a kennel."

Fuck me.

Stalking back inside, he swiped the envelope off the table and broke the seal before he registered that Beatrix was no longer there. "What the bloody hell—?"

4

His entire body folded in on itself, twisting and compacting until he was no more than a speck of dust in the air. And then, as if the world's largest vacuum cleaner had suddenly turned on, he flew. Over the lights of London, the black nothingness of the Atlantic Ocean, the eastern seaboard of the United States, until he found himself in the middle of Bourbon Street, New Orleans, where with a subtle *pop*, he was suddenly returned to his original form.

"Fucking magic."

MADDOX

The celestial realm was *boring*.

Maddox leaned against a pillar in Azrael's foyer, waiting for the Angel of Death to grant him an audience. Even here, where archangels came and went frequently, ferrying souls —some willing, some very unwilling to leave their bodies— to the realm, he still couldn't muster the enthusiasm to care.

His immortal life stretched out before him, endless time he couldn't break into hours or days like his brother could. Sinclair had been banished hundreds of years ago, consigned to Hell for a century after his part in one of the most depraved crime sprees the world had ever known.

Prohibited from returning to the celestial realm and made to live among humans on earth, Sinclair was trying to atone for his sins, but, his ledger was weighted so far to the negative that it would take him a thousand human lifetimes or more to even be able to visit Maddox for a short time. His soul had been fractured into pieces, and only a very small part of it remained within his body. The rest...lost to the demons who'd used him, controlled him, and forced him to do their bidding.

Maddox missed Sinclair. They'd grown up together, earned their wings together. Once Sinclair had been released from Hell, Maddox had been able to visit him. They'd walked among the humans so Maddox could experience the earthen realm. He'd tried alcohol, watched a football match, and enjoyed something called a movie.

Unlike Maddox, who was half angel and half human, Sinclair's angelic parentage was mixed with that of a demon. A succubus, to be exact, making Sin an incubus. And while Mad had watched, Sinclair had fed from half a dozen humans, taking their sexual energy and leaving them with pleasant or thrilling memories.

He never took from anyone unwilling. One of the conditions of his sentence—but also something so very ingrained within Sin's personality after what he'd been made to endure, he could not possibly do anything else.

When he required energy, he'd glamour a human into ducking into an alley or a closet with him, search their minds for their deepest sexual fantasies, and use those thoughts as his meal. If the unsuspecting human kissed Sin, all the better, but it wasn't required. And when he was done, he wiped their memories and replaced them with something happy.

Maddox didn't need sexual energy, but he'd been so curious, he'd chatted up several humans, both males and females, and even kissed two of them—one of each sex. He much preferred the male human to the female.

"Both men and women are sexual beings, Mad," Sinclair said as he and Maddox walked down a busy street in Seattle after spending time in what was called a pub. "I can take from either, but I prefer those of the female persuasion."

"I felt nothing kissing the woman," Maddox replied. He'd been so disappointed in his first kiss, he'd almost left the pub and returned to the celestial realm immediately, but Sinclair had urged him to talk to a few men before he left, and the last one... he'd been delicious. Maddox's dick—which he'd never given much thought to while in the celestial realm—had hardened, and a deep ache had started in his balls.

And then he'd been called back to the celestial realm by a very impatient Azrael, who demanded to know why Maddox had been about to have sex with a human. It wasn't exactly...forbidden, but highly frowned upon. One too many angels had succumbed to human temptation and decided never to return, and Azrael, one of the few who could grant access to the earthen realm, was tired of losing his angels to earth.

Mad sighed as he watched another soul struggle in an archangel's grip, wailing, "I want to go back! I don't want to die!"

Why would any soul want to return to a body that was decaying? Sin had talked about pain. About how he'd been injured while working for a human law enforcement agency. How earthen bodies took time to heal. As a half-demon, half-angel, Sin healed quickly, but humans often did not.

And they aged. Broke down. Could not move quickly or without pops and creaks and...*noises.* Maddox would have to ask Azrael one day why a soul would not want to be free from pain. Or, perhaps the souls simply knew how completely devoid of *fun* the celestial realm was.

A golden door burst open, and the Angel of Death strode across the foyer. "If you want an audience, Maddox, you will follow me. I have little time."

Mad trailed behind Azrael, into a sparkling, lavish bathing chamber with a bubbling fount in the center. Azrael shed his robes and stepped into the water, his corded muscles flexing with each small movement.

Unprepared, Maddox gaped at the pure beauty of the angel, and under his robes, his member started to throb. Quickly, he clasped his hands in front of himself and stared at a point over Azrael's head until the angel was submerged up to his neck. "Well?"

"I wish to ask for an indulgence."

Azrael waved one of his hands—he currently only had two, but they multiplied when he was recording the various births and deaths on earth—urging Maddox to get on with it.

"Sinclair. His sentence in the earthen realm may never end without assistance."

The angel's eyes narrowed. "And you think *you* can help him with his redemption?"

"There must be something I can do." Maddox took a step closer to the fount, but that only revealed more of Azrael's defined muscles, and so he kept his eyes downcast. "I...miss him."

"Sinclair will return to the celestial realm when he is ready. His sentence has nothing to do with time. Only with the clearing of his soul's mark."

"Then tell me how I can help him clear the mark."

The frustrated sound rumbling in Azrael's chest, along with the jerk of his wings sent Maddox stepping back in fear. No one crossed Azrael. Making him angry was a very good way to find yourself assigned to Purgatory.

After a moment, the Angel of Death sighed. "There is something I require. An item stolen from our realm and in the possession of a coven of witches in a place called *New Orleans*."

"I can retrieve it for you," Maddox said, hope building deep inside him. "Anything. What is it?"

"A vial of celestial sand from the shores of the Sea of Redemption. With it, the witches have power over life and death, a power no human should ever be able to wield. Find it and bring it back to me, and I will see what I can do about your brother."

Maddox bowed, his wings dipping and touching the ground as he backed away. "Thank you, Azrael. Your kindness knows no bounds."

"You may not think me so kind when you land in the human realm," the angel muttered. "I have heard nothing good about this *New Orleans*. A den of sin and iniquity. See the Traveler before you leave. He will provide you with appropriate clothing and a token for your return. Now be gone. This is the only time I have to myself, and I would like to enjoy it."

Maddox spun on his heel and sprinted from the room. By the time he'd left Azrael's dominion, he was floating two feet above the ground, his wings fluttering softly in air that was always the perfect temperature, smelled like the freshest breeze, and cushioned every fall.

He was going to the earthen realm. To New Orleans. And he was finally going to be able to help Sinclair return where he belonged.

CHAPTER TWO

KILLIAN

The crowds were going to drive him mad. Or cause him to lose control. Killian fingered the cuff around his wrist, praying his emotions would not overwhelm the dampening spell infused into the metal before he got somewhere...quiet.

But where?

Beatrix could have warned him. Or Tiny. That damn cat had known there was magic in the envelope. "No more tuna for you," he muttered to no one.

Glancing down at the invitation, he frowned.

Killian Wade

You are invited to the Gathering

Magnolia House, Samhain Eve

As he read, the words shifted.

You will be met at the Monarch Hotel. All you require will be provided.

Fucking spelled ink. He didn't even have his mobile on

him. And with the dampening cuff, he could not summon it. Not unless he wanted to risk the lives of the hundreds of people around him.

Scanning the street, he spied a police officer watching the crowds. Certainly he would know where this hotel was. "Pardon me," Killian said as he approached slowly. "I'm afraid I've gotten myself all turned around. Would you be able to direct me to the Monarch Hotel?"

The officer peered down at him—the man had to be half a head taller than Killian—and frowned. "How much have you had to drink tonight, sir?"

"Nothing. Why?"

Arching a brow, the police officer nodded toward the corner. "Because the Monarch Hotel is all of thirty feet away."

"Bugger it," Killian said as he sighed and gave a small shake of his head. "My better half is right. She can't take me anywhere. I have no sense of direction. Apologies. When I tell her how daft I was that I couldn't see what was right in front of me, she'll never let me live it down."

The cop's lips twitched into a half-smile. "I won't tell her. Just...don't get yourself in any trouble."

"No, sir. Not at all. Good night." Killian rushed across the street, weaving through a parade of revelers wearing all manner of costumes, until he could push through the doors of the Monarch Hotel.

The scent of jasmine floated over the air, along with a hint of spice and sandalwood. The lobby was done up in rich paneling, thick golden and burgundy carpets, with antique lights hanging from the ceiling.

In a far corner, seated in a wing-back chair with her long legs crossed, a slit in her dress all the way up her thigh, was the one witch Killian had hoped to never see again.

Jezebel Winters. She drummed her perfectly manicured fingernails on the side table, a bored expression plastered on her heart-shaped face. "About damn time, Killian," she said as he approached.

Of course it would be her.

Rising, she offered him her hand, and he brought it to his lips. "Jezebel. I suppose I have you to thank for this *generous* invitation?"

Oliver's sister had wanted Killian burned alive for his crimes, but Beatrix had intervened. The favors many in the magical community owed her had saved Killian's life.

"Puh-leeze. You think I *wanted* you here? I'd just as soon never see your face again. Delphine ordered me to meet you. Something about learning to hold my tongue in a public place." She snorted. "My *tongue* isn't the problem."

Raising her hand, she slid her fingers over the pad of her thumb. Once. Twice. Three times. Each time, faster. A tiny glow started in the palm of her hand, and as she kept up the movement, it brightened until Killian had to look away or lose his sight.

"Jezebel, please," he hissed as he glanced around the empty hotel lobby. "Someone could see you."

"Do you think I care, Killian? You *killed my twin.* My other half. The only being I hate more in this world than you is the vampire who turned him in the first place. I want the both of you to burn. Instead, I'm playing errand-girl for Delphine because for some idiotic reason, you're *here.*" The disdain dripped from every word, and with the ball of magic still hovering above her palm, Killian's heart started to pound so hard, he could feel it all the way up his neck and into his temples.

With her free hand, she shoved a small envelope at him.

"Room 13. Clothes, toiletries, everything you need is in there. Now...run."

She didn't need to tell him twice. He took off at a sprint down the hall, but he wasn't fast enough. The blast of magic hit him in the shoulder, sending him tumbling face first onto the thick carpet.

For a few panicked seconds, he couldn't breathe. The world seemed to slow and took on a faint shimmer. And then she stood over him. Looking down like he was something to be pitied. Or hated. He couldn't tell.

"Next time, run faster," she said, then snapped her fingers, breaking whatever spell she'd cast over him, and disappeared.

In New Orleans for less than ten minutes, and already he'd almost died. What other fucked up Hell did the Universe have in store for him tonight? Trudging towards his room, he shook his head. He didn't want to know.

A LITTLE OVER AN HOUR LATER, Killian examined himself in the full-length mirror. He'd shaved the stubble he favored, even styled his hair a bit so it no longer hung over his forehead. The black bespoke suit fit him perfectly, but then again, everything in this suite was tailored expressly for him.

His favorite soap. The expensive Savile Row shampoo. A straight razor, sharpened to lethality. The black, button-down shirt with the flattened collar, the black tie, even the shoes, polished so he could see his reflection in them.

On the dresser, he found a platinum Rolex, a fully charged mobile, and his wallet, but no passport.

"Bugger." Getting him here was one thing. He hoped whoever was pulling his strings had some way to return him home. Because without his passport, he wasn't leaving the States. Not unless he relied on his magic. And using magic? That was out of the question.

~

MADDOX

New Orleans was wet. The air felt thick, like Maddox was breathing underwater. It was also warm. He'd been here all of one human hour and already he had to mop his brow. The white suit, black loafers, and feathered mask the Traveler had assigned to him felt restrictive compared to his usual attire of robes and sandals.

He could not decide if he liked this place. It was *real*. Gritty. There were smells everywhere. Food. Sweat. Cologne. Piss. So many they were almost overwhelming.

"Your human side will take over while you are in the earthen realm, Maddox. While you should retain your immortality for the short period you are there, you can be injured, and you will take time to heal. You will hunger and thirst, want for things you have never imagined before. You remember this from your visit with your brother?" The Traveler crossed his arms over his chest as he looked Maddox up and down.

"Yes. I *very much enjoyed food. And bourbon."* Maddox buttoned his white coat and stretched his wings to their fullest. The clothing was specially designed to allow them to move, to be free, but the Traveler waved his finger at Maddox.

"You are not to use your wings in front of humans. They will not understand. Your time in the earthen realm should be short, so you will not need to hide them completely. It is Samhain, and all of the humans will be in costumes. Simply keep them folded at your back."

"Of course." Maddox *fingered the token in his pocket. "I won't disappoint Azrael. I will retrieve the vial and return as quickly as I can. But...after that, will I be allowed to contact Sinclair and tell him—"*

The Traveler arched a brow. "Azrael will decide that upon your return."

A crowd passed him by, singing and dancing in a long line as they made their way down the sidewalk. Maddox reached out with his gifts to sense them. He was a lesser angel. Incapable of working miracles. But he could sample a human's emotions. Joy. Happiness. Relief. As he wove his way through the throngs of people toward Magnolia House, the location of the vial he was supposed to retrieve, he found everyone he touched—in the spiritual sense—carried these same emotions.

And the colors. So many colors. He'd researched Samhain, and this behavior was typical. People dressed up in costumes and masks, fanciful dresses, as terrifying creatures, and even animals, yet they were all still enjoying themselves.

"Nice wings, bro!" A man slapped him on the shoulder, and Maddox almost lost control and took off into the sky to get away, but after he caught sight of the reveler—who wore a bright red suit with white trim and a fat, black belt—he relaxed.

"Thank you...Santa." Despite Maddox's lack of experience on earth, he knew of Santa Claus. The *real* St. Nicholas would never step foot in New Orleans, but this Santa was obviously inebriated, and while his slap had stung, it had done no permanent harm.

Perhaps he *should* have chosen to hide his wings. He could fold them tightly against his back, use his gifts to hide them from view, even withdraw them into his body completely, though that was uncomfortable for long periods of time. Except he was headed into a gathering of the earthen realm's most powerful witches, and he would need all of his strength should anything go wrong.

With every step he took closer to Magnolia House, he could sense more of the magic the New Orleans coven used to protect themselves. It was an overly sweet taste in his mouth. The spells weren't purely evil, but they weren't completely good either. Something felt...wrong about the undercurrents some of the spells carried.

How in all of the many realms had the coven obtained celestial sand? The Sea of Redemption was always calm, always the perfect temperature, and the sand could heal any injury. Any pain. That was one of the reasons the sand was valued. It was powerful enough to bring humans back to life.

No angel would ever have simply offered a vial to a human. Any human. One of the witches must have visited the celestial realm somehow.

After turning down another block, Maddox stopped and gawked up at Magnolia House.

A short, iron fence wrapped around the large property, and every inch of the building glowed with thousands of lights hung from the eaves, attached to every tree, and lining the massive veranda in front of the structure.

A few witches already milled about, but Maddox had timed his arrival so he would be inside before the official start of the ball. Azrael had told him stories of what happened here. Drinking, dancing, debauchery...all were allowed on Samhain. Encouraged, even.

Maddox wished he could stay for the festivities. Experience something *real*. Something *fun*. Then again, he was breaking into a locked crypt, in the basement of a place where any of the witches he encountered could and would cause him great pain.

Or worse. They could prevent him from ever returning to the celestial realm. The Traveler had warned him. Torture. Imprisonment. Endless agony.

"Do not linger, Maddox. Get the vial and get out."

Slipping around the back of the mansion, he found an unattended door. From the aromas that escaped, it led directly to the kitchen.

Staff rushed around, filling platters with appetizers, chilling Champagne, and icing cakes. Mad sent a small burst of his angelic power through the room, ensuring none of the humans would notice him as he crept through and into a richly appointed hallway.

Creamy paint, dark wood, and fine art lined the walls. His shoes made light tapping sounds on the shiny wooden floors. With his palm trailing along the smooth rail, he hurried down the stairs to the basement, through another door, along a more utilitarian hallway this time, and around a corner.

The crypt.

Runes, both carved and burned, covered the thick wooden doors, and Maddox held out his hand, sensing the magic. It pushed against him, resisting, until he withdrew the celestial token Azrael had given him. Sending his energy into the golden coin, he watched as the runes shifted and transformed. The heavy door opened with an eerie creaking sound, and the scent of old bones invaded his nose.

Candles flickered all around the room, and in alcoves built into every wall rested ornate glass and gold chests, vials, and relics, both religious and secular, Wiccan and Pagan. Maddox crossed the threshold, and a spell wrapped around him, threatening his steps, but he shook it off and started searching for the celestial sand.

Every minute that passed ratcheted his nerves.

Go faster.

But he couldn't. The relics called to him, demanded his respect and awe. So much so that they must have been spelled. He lost track of time until he caught a sparkle out of the corner of his eye. In three steps, he stood in front of a small alcove no more than seven inches tall with the vial of sand resting on a red satin pillow.

The moment his fingers curled around the small glass vessel, he felt its power, and he tucked it into the inner pocket of his jacket, turned, and fled from the room.

CHAPTER THREE

KILLIAN

The New Orleans Coven knew how to throw a party. He'd give them that. Magnolia House, with its old world opulence of marble and carved wood railings, richly colored wallpaper, and polished floors that must have been spelled, for even with hundreds of witches in attendance, there wasn't a speck of dust or dirt on them, welcomed all.

Fires burned in every hearth, and the antique light fixtures sparkled. Conversations bubbled up around him, and Killian caught snippets from time to time, including several young female witches who wanted a snog—or a roll in the sheets—with him.

"Champagne, sir?" A server in a black suit held a tray of glasses, and Killian snagged a flute before wandering towards the ballroom. An empty alcove provided a convenient place for him to stay out of the way and scan the crowds. Something about this night sat ill with him—beyond the oddness of his invitation—and he fingered the cuff around his wrist, ensuring it was firmly in place. The last thing he needed was his magic going sideways on him before he could figure out why Delphine had demanded his presence.

From this vantage point, he could see all the way out to the garden, which was filled with cocktail tables draped with dark blue cloths, a spelled ball of golden light hovering above each one. Impervious to the wind whispering through the trees, the light danced, illuminating the witches, mortals, and otherworldly creatures in attendance.

Lingering close to the edge of the garden, Natalie spotted him, and Killian groaned to himself. The witch had made a play for him the only other time they'd been in the same room, and he'd been so flustered, he'd failed to mention that he played for the other team. If he brought it up now, she'd think him a proper dolt.

As if gliding on a cloud of air, Delphine, the New Orleans Coven High Priestess passed by his hiding place, and Killian raised his glass, hoping a healthy sip of the bubbly would give him the courage to confront her.

Until the wind turned cold, bitter, and harsh, and Killian stopped with the flute of champagne halfway to his lips. Under the din of conversation, he heard a harsh, cruel voice chanting.

"'Neath silver moon or dark of night.
"In shadow deep or brightest light.
"From this hex none shall be spared.
"For wrath knows not peace nor care.
"Betrayers! Gather close and hear.
"I damn you to your darkest fear.

"I bind you to dread's cold embrace.

"Until your truth you boldly face."

Greenish curls of smoke rolled in from the garden, winding around Killian's ankles and cementing him in place. His heart seemed to freeze as well, his breath caught in his chest. In the doorway, Delphine swayed on her feet, her mouth open slightly in shock.

Endless seconds passed, the terror rising inside of him, until a percussive force shook the entire mansion, knocking him to the ground where he fell on top of his champagne flute.

A sharp stab of pain lanced through his abdomen, and his ears rang, the screams and shouts all around him muffled as he tried to right himself. Delphine staggered to her feet and took off for the stairs, lurching with every step.

Something sticky dripped from his ears, and when he touched his cheek, his fingers came away wet with blood. Burning pain stretched across his chest, a thin line of agony he clutched at while he tried to stand.

His first step sent his shoulder slamming into the wall. His arms and legs were heavy and leaden, and as he fumbled for the piece of glass that had impaled him just above his belt, a chill of foreboding washed over him. Along with pain in his wrist like he'd never felt before.

He tugged the sleeve of his jacket up.

Fuck me.

His cuff turned to dust that floated to the ground in a slow-motion spiral. Magic crackled over his skin, electric and hot, and he pushed himself off the wall and started to run.

If he stayed in this mansion another moment, he was a danger to everyone. Hell, the entire city of New Orleans should be as afraid of his magic as he was.

MADDOX

He stumbled up the stairs, blind, his wings flapping uselessly as he tried to get his bearings. Where was he? Nothing made any sense. His head hurt like someone had driven a spike through it, and he banged into more than one person as he tried to fight his way to where he *thought* the door might be.

He'd been so close. Almost halfway up the stairs, but then his entire world had stopped, and he hadn't been able to breathe, to move. Nothing.

When the mansion had shook like God herself was trying to bring it down, the paralysis had disappeared, but it had taken his vision and most of his hearing with it.

His feathers bent, and a bone in his left wing snapped as he tried to escape. The pain stole his breath, but then fresh air hit his cheeks. He still couldn't see, could only hear a dull roar in his ears. More than once, he fell, scraping his hands on the stone steps just outside the mansion.

The scent of his own blood turned his stomach, and as he pushed to his feet, bright lights broke up the darkness. Several of the humans screamed and shoved at him, and Maddox found himself turned around, dizzy and disoriented.

His foot slipped off the curb, and he flapped his wings again, but with one of them broken, he only managed to spin himself around in a circle. A car horn blared, white-hot light seared his eyes, and then he flew.

But not in the way he'd intended. Pure, unadulterated agony ran through his limbs, his back, and his chest from an impact like he'd never felt before, and when he hit the ground after a screech of tires and a man's curse, he tried to get back up, but he couldn't move. It wasn't only his wing now. His arm, several ribs, even his collarbone were broken too. His legs. He tried to shift them, but let out an agonized cry when he could do nothing but flop around helplessly.

The last vestiges of darkness cleared from his eyes, and he stared up at the inky sky, at the full moon overhead.

He didn't think he could die—not after only a few hours in the earthen realm, but his body hurt—so much—that he feared he was wrong. And even if he lived...he couldn't move. If the witches found him with the sand, they'd torture him for the rest of his existence.

Footsteps. So many footsteps. All around him. Maddox reached out with his good arm and wrapped his fingers around an ankle. "Help," he whispered.

The owner of the ankle tried to shake off his hold, but then stopped. "Fuck." A second later, the most perfect face he'd ever seen hovered over him, and the man pressed warm fingers to his neck. A spark ran through Maddox from his head to his toes, and his entire body started to tremble. "You're hurt, mate. Don't move. I can't stay, but I'll call an ambulance for you. They'll be here soon."

"N-no," Maddox begged, snagging the stranger's wrist in a weak grip. "P-please. Do not...leave me."

Piercing blue-gray eyes held his, and Maddox tried to use his gifts, tried to sense the man's emotions, but he felt nothing. No warmth deep inside of him. No connection to the Divine. To the celestial realm.

"Can't...go to hospital. Look." Maddox moved his right shoulder, extending the tip of his wing.

"Bloody hell," the stranger muttered. "I can't get involved in this, angel. If I do, I'll be the death of you, and I am *not* going to have an angel's end on my hands." He started to rise, and an arc of light and power leapt from the man's heart and hit Maddox in the chest.

The shock sent Mad's body into convulsions, and he tasted blood. Warm hands cupped his cheeks. "Breathe, angel. Slowly. In and out." As Maddox focused on the man's voice and the kindness in his eyes, he managed to calm his body, but he still couldn't move.

"Please..."

"I wish I could help, but I have to get somewhere far away from here before I hurt people. That bolt of magic? That was nothing."

"Find the intruder!" a woman shrieked into the night, her words carrying over all of the screams around them. "Find the vial!"

The intruder. Him. Torture. Imprisonment. Death. Maddox barely managed to grunt what he feared would be his last free words in his long, supposedly immortal life.

"Left...jacket pocket. They'll destroy me...for taking it. Hide it, at least."

"This is a terrible idea," the man said as he reached into Maddox's pocket. "Fuck." Jerking his hand back, he stared at the blood coating his fingers and the broken vial of celestial sand, a few grains of which landed on Maddox's chest and infused him with a subtle warmth, turning the complete agony of his injuries into a more manageable torment.

Pulling a handkerchief from his pocket, his potential savior wrapped the vial tightly and tucked it away. "I am going to regret this. What's your name, angel?"

"Maddox." The word escaped so quietly, it was only a whisper, and darkness encroached around the edges of his vision.

"Killian. Killian Wade. If my magic kills you, Maddox, put in a good word for me. I do not fancy spending eternity in Hell."

As Killian slid his arm behind Mad's back, the agony

consumed him, every breath more painful than the last, and once he found himself cradled against his rescuer's chest, he let go, falling into the void of unconsciousness—or death— thinking how good Killian smelled, and how he wished he could stay with him.

CHAPTER FOUR

KILLIAN

A fucking angel? The man in his arms barely made a sound as Killian ducked down an alley on the way back to the Monarch Hotel. He'd saddled himself with an angel. And worse yet, one who apparently wasn't as immortal as Killian had always thought they would be. The man's hands were scraped and bleeding, one of his wings was bent, and his body shuddered with every breath.

The line of fire currently consuming Killian's chest magnified, curling upwards towards his neck. What in the bloody hell had the curse done to him besides take away his most precious possession and leave him a danger to everyone. He groaned as he tightened his hold on Maddox. If he wasn't careful, he'd drop the angel, and he didn't know how much more Maddox could take.

Just before he burst out onto Bourbon Street, Killian peered around the corner. Shite. There had to be two hundred people between him and his hotel. Two hundred people who'd see him carrying a bloody man with breathtaking white wings folded against his back. Couldn't angels hide the damn things?

Well, it *was* Samhain. The wings probably wouldn't get a second glance. The blood, however...

"If I blow a hole in the eastern seaboard," he said to Maddox quietly, "I'm blaming you." The last time he'd tried to use any sort of magic, he'd fried his fingers to a crisp. And now, without his cuff, he had no way to control his power.

His head still ached from the curse, and he could feel the blood from his ears drying on his neck. Killian closed his eyes, his back pressed to the wall of a squat building. The magic started as a spark inside him, warming, growing, until it was a living, breathing energy fighting to be free.

"Mark this place and stop its time. Fleet of foot and smooth of tongue, let us pass unseen among."

The sounds of Bourbon Street faded into silence, and when Killian risked a glance, every single living thing—man, woman, child, dog, and even mosquito—had frozen in place. It was the first spell he'd tried in years that hadn't destroyed everything around him.

Only pausing for a moment to wonder why he'd gotten so lucky, Killian took off at a slow jog—all he could manage with the solidly build angel in his arms—and wove among the frozen people, ducking and twisting, until he came to the hotel. Pushing against the door with his back, he almost fell into the lobby, but even here, everyone was completely still.

Not until he reached Room 13 did he release the spell, and the after-effects hit him like a sledge hammer. He barely got Maddox to the bed before Killian dropped to his knees, grabbing his head with a mournful, inhuman howl.

Clawing his way to the window, he parted the curtains. Out on Bourbon Street, people continued to celebrate

Samhain, and Killian fell back down with a choking sob. He'd done it. Cast a spell, released it, and hadn't killed anyone. Thank the Divine.

From the bed, Maddox coughed weakly, and Killian got to his knees, fighting off the dizziness to crawl back to the bed.

Was this why he'd been summoned to New Orleans? To be hit by this blasted curse and get himself entangled with an angel? He did not know who'd cast the spell or why, but the words were burned into his brain.

"Betrayers! Gather close and hear.

"I damn you to your darkest fear.

"I bind you to dread's cold embrace.

"Until your truth you boldly face."

Killian hadn't betrayed anyone. Except for Oliver. Fuck. If the curse was going to punish him for that crime, it might as well kill him now. Except for the angel bleeding on his bed. Killian pulled himself out of his own pity party and stared at Maddox. His skin was ruddy, a layer of stubble darkening his jaw and cheeks under the blood that had dried on his temple.

Black hair, thick and wavy, had felt impossibly soft as Killian had tucked Maddox's head under his chin while carrying him. And the man—was he a man?—was muscular and compact. Like a fighter.

As he stared, the angel stirred and forced his eyes open. "Help...me," Maddox whispered. "Killian?"

"I'm right here, mate." Sliding a hip onto the bed, Killian rested his hand on Maddox's shoulder. A burst of warmth flowed through him, and across his chest, his burns flared. "Fuck," he muttered as he used his other hand to loosen his tie. His abdomen throbbed with each breath, and now that he wasn't in the throes of an adrenaline spike, all of his injuries started to make themselves known as well.

Maddox's cheeks reddened, then paled dramatically as he tried to shift on the bed. "Have...to set my...wing. My arm. Before they heal badly."

"Will you be all right for five minutes?" If he didn't do something about the burning in his chest and the slice from the shattered champagne flute, he wouldn't be any good to anyone—especially Maddox. And the man seemed to be in complete agony.

Maddox's lips moved, but Killian couldn't make out his response. Leaning closer, he caught Maddox's scent. Something clean and pure and very male. Granite and leather and the finest tobacco. "I didn't hear you, Maddox."

"Think so."

Pushing to his feet with a groan, Killian stumbled into the suite's bath and tore his shirt open. "Bloody hell." Blazing across his chest, almost like a tattoo, were several curved lines etched into his skin. On his left side, one stretched from his sternum, over his pectoral muscle, almost to his collarbone. Several others looked almost like half-moons running directly under the long curve. On the right, dark triangles overlapped. Each mark glowed red around the edges, like he'd been branded with a hot poker.

As he stared, another black dot seared itself into his flesh, and he bit down on one of the hotel towels to stop from crying out. *No more. Give me ten minutes. For Maddox.*

His bargain with the Divine must have worked, because the pain faded, and the new dot didn't grow or change shape.

His dress shirt fell to the floor, and he pressed his fingers to the deep gash just below his ribs. Blood still dripped from the wound, and he rummaged around in the toiletry bag *someone* had been kind enough to fill for him until he found gauze, medical tape, and a tube of antibiotic ointment.

"Convenient, that," he said to his reflection in the mirror. "And definitely not standard issue."

Unwilling to even touch the new brand, he cleaned the gash with an alcohol-soaked pad, hissing at the pain, slathered it with ointment, and wrapped it tightly. Then, he gathered up all of the supplies—including a suture kit— filled a glass of water, and headed back to Maddox.

~

MADDOX

He had to be seeing things. The gorgeous man heading towards him had dark, angry lines tattooed on his chest, and they seemed to glow with each step. Killian's six-pack ended in a deep *v* that disappeared beneath his black pants, and a patch of brilliant white gauze on his side was tinged with red.

"You're hurt." Maddox forced the words through gritted teeth, reaching his one good arm up to brush his fingers against Killian's side.

"I'll live. Will you?" Killian's blue-grey eyes softened as he stared down at Maddox. "I'll help you. But which, err, wing is broken?"

"My left. Same arm. A few ribs. Collarbone, I think." Maddox was so thirsty, so weak, and he didn't think he could stay conscious much longer. But he didn't want to stop staring at Killian. There was something about the man that called to him, and it wasn't just that he was hot as fuck.

Killian slid his arm behind Maddox, and they were so close, the man's warmth enveloped him. It was...comforting. Something he could hold on to...for at least a short while. Until Killian lifted him, and his broken arm and wing flopped helplessly to his side, sending pure, unadulterated torment shooting through his entire body.

"Keep it down, mate," Killian said sharply as he eased Maddox against his chest and slid behind him to rest his back against the headboard. "We're not the only guests in this hotel."

Had he screamed? His throat hurt like he'd screamed, but he couldn't remember. He must have. Letting his head rest on Killian's shoulder, Maddox tried to breathe through his misery until the cool edge of a glass pressed to his lips.

"Drink. Slowly." After three sips, Maddox felt marginally better, and Killian set the glass down. "I know nothing of setting bones. Or of...angels. I thought your kind were immortal."

"S'posed to be." Maddox was so tired, he was having a hard time keeping his eyes open. "Even on earth. Should have...healed by now. Ever since the mansion..."

"Bloody hell. The curse hit you too. Did you see green smoke? Before everything went sideways?"

"Smoke. Yes," Maddox whispered. "Couldn't move."

"That vial. You *stole* it from Magnolia House, didn't you?" Despite his words, Killian's tone hadn't changed. If anything, it had gentled, and Maddox didn't want to lie to this man. The intense urge to tell him everything didn't make sense, but nor could he dismiss it.

"Yes. I was on the stairs. Everything," he shuddered, and Killian's arm tightened across his chest, "stopped. I couldn't breathe." Maddox groaned and stared down at his broken arm, bent oddly at his side. "Like I was...frozen. And then, darkness. I don't know how I got out. Didn't see anything until...the car."

"Someone at the witches' ball cursed the lot of us," Killian said quietly. "I can't stay long here, Maddox. I'm a danger to you. Help me figure out what to do about your injuries, and then you can have the room. It's paid up for two more days. But if I don't get far away from people soon, even your celestial strength won't save you."

Maddox fought through the pain, almost passing out more than once as Killian removed his white shirt. But as soon as the bare skin of his back and his wings rested against Killian's chest, he started to feel better. The contact settled him. Eased his fears over what Azrael would say when he found out the vial had broken. He had to ask Killian to give it back to him.

"All right. Bite down, Maddox." Killian folded his belt in half and eased it between Maddox's teeth. "This is going to hurt."

By the time Killian had bound his arm tightly, set his wing using one of the pillow cases torn into strips, and cleaned the various scrapes and scratches on his hands and face, Maddox didn't know which way was up. He just wanted Killian's arms around him again.

"Stay," he whispered when Killian covered him with a blanket. Maddox threaded his fingers with his rescuer's and held on. "Please. Don't leave."

Killian's response was lost as sleep wrapped Maddox in a warm embrace, but he thought he felt the man squeeze his hand, and that brought him a measure of peace.

CHAPTER FIVE

KILLIAN

H e should have left. But the angel's hand on his brought about such an intense wave of connection and desire, he couldn't walk away. Instead, he sat next to Maddox for hours. Every time he tried to let go, something stopped him.

His mind raced. Had he been summoned to New Orleans specifically to be cursed? From the other witches running around dazed, all bleeding from their ears, noses, and some even their eyes, the curse had hit the lot of them. If Maddox had been affected too, what about all the other supernatural creatures present tonight?

The woman who'd uttered those vile words...he'd recognized her voice. Somewhere deep in his memories. But for all his efforts, he could not place it now. Pulling out his wallet, he extracted the only photo he had left of Oliver. Of the two of them together. They'd been almost inseparable since birth, and when Oliver had run afoul of a vampire and had been turned, only Killian's sleeping schedule changed. He started staying up until all hours so he and Oliver could spend time together. Until that terrible moonless night when Killian had tried to protect his closest friend, the man he'd shared his first kiss with, the man he'd been about to take as a lover, from a werewolf with a grudge and a silver dagger.

Killian's eyes burned as the memories assaulted him. Oliver's last seconds of existence. The look of betrayal in his eyes. The sorrow. How Killian had tried to save him. Pulled him off the fence and used a healing spell, only to have that magic burn away what remained of his would-be-lover's heart rather than healing it.

And for ten years, Killian hadn't used his magic unless he was alone at his estate. Even then, he only tried when Tiny managed to goad him into it. And now, he was unprotected. As was Maddox.

Eventually, he managed to extricate his fingers from Maddox's grip and curled up in the wing-back chair in the corner of the suite, a blanket draped over his bare chest, watching the man sleep. There was a vulnerability about the angel that tugged at Killian's soul, and despite the magic that threatened to burst from his fingertips every time he took a deep breath, he couldn't leave, no matter how much he wanted to.

You only need to ensure he makes it through the night. Once the sun rises, get the fuck out, find Delphine, and figure out why the hell she summoned you here.

He owed the angel nothing. So why then, was he so drawn to the man? On the table next to him, the broken vial with a scant tablespoon of sparkling sand drew his focus. Maddox had been acutely afraid of someone finding it, of the witches knowing he'd taken it. Yet he trusted Killian?

Gingerly lifting the vessel, he turned it around and around, sniffed it, and frowned. What the hell was it? And why would the New Orleans coven want it?

From the bed, Maddox groaned, and Killian sat up a little straighter, his back protesting the odd positions he'd contorted himself into all night at the angel's side.

"Maddox?" Killian said softly. If the man wasn't fully awake, he didn't want to startle him. In fact, he almost wished Maddox would sleep another day...or two...just so Killian wouldn't have to leave him.

Get over yourself. He's an angel. And you're...probably going to Hell.

"Where am I?" Maddox asked as he pushed up on an elbow, winced, and fell back against the pillows again. "Who...?"

"Killian. You're in my bed." He immediately regretted the statement when Maddox's cheeks flushed a deep pink. "Not like that. You were hit by a car. Remember?"

"Oh, fuck." Maddox pulled the blanket up higher, tucking it under his good arm.

"I did not expect an angel to swear." Killian limped over to the bed and eased himself down. The wound to his side still throbbed, but at least the new marks across his chest were no longer causing him agony with each beat of his heart. "Here." Holding a glass of water to Maddox's full lips, Killian willed his dick to calm the fuck down. An angel was *the last* kind of man Killian should want. Especially now.

"I'm only half-angel." Maddox used his good arm to angle himself higher, hissed out a breath, and then grabbed onto Killian. The bolt of electricity that arced between the two shocked them both, but Maddox didn't let go.

"Take it easy." He wasn't certain why he cared so much about the half-angel, but the idea of seeing Maddox in pain didn't sit well with Killian. "And the other half?" Killian gently guided Maddox so he was sitting mostly upright, his back against the pillows.

"Human." Maddox extended his arm tentatively. "It still hurts."

"You broke your arm. Humans take six to eight weeks to heal from something like that. You shouldn't even be able to move it yet."

"I think I will heal in no more than two days. My brother, he's trapped in the earthen realm, and he is often injured in his job. But he heals quickly."

Running a hand through his dark brown hair, Killian tried to figure out what he was supposed to do with the angel now. "Do you think you can stand?"

"Maybe." Pushing the sheet down to his waist, Maddox threw his legs over the side of the bed while Killian's gaze was drawn equally to the deep bruises across the angel's abdomen and his sculpted muscles. Thank the Divine nothing below Maddox's waist had been broken, he'd be sporting a full stiffy.

Stepping back to give his patient some room—and when did he start thinking of Maddox as *his*?—Killian shoved his hands into his pockets, then immediately regretted the gesture when Maddox toppled into him.

"Maybe not." The angel shuddered, and Killian wrapped an arm around his waist. "But, uh...I really need to..." He nodded towards the suite's bathroom.

"Another thing I did not expect angels to do. Then again, if you're half human..." Killian guided him until Maddox could lean against the counter on his own. "I'll be outside," he said as he backed away and shut the door.

Taking the few minutes to himself, Killian strode over to the closet. It had been stocked with clothing that fit him perfectly, and he chose a fresh shirt in a light blue and eased it over his aching shoulders.

What the fuck was he supposed to do now? He couldn't leave Maddox alone if the man couldn't even get himself to the bathroom and back. Sparks danced across Killian's fingers, landing on his black pants and burning holes in the material.

Patting his thighs to put out the smoldering embers, Killian strode over to the ice bucket and shoved both of his hands inside. The frigid, mostly melted water made his fingers ache, but at least his magic couldn't escape and burn down the entire hotel.

Beatrix would know what to do. Why the fuck hadn't he thought to call her the previous night?

Because you were preoccupied with the angel in your bed.

She understood Killian's unique...challenges. And though she'd never been supportive of him hiding away from the world, she hadn't insisted he join the coven for their weekly meetings either. She'd help.

But just as he pulled out his mobile, Maddox emerged from the bathroom, a little unsteady but otherwise upright. "Where's the vial, Killian? I need it back. Right now. Then I have to get out of here. Back to the celestial realm or Azrael will murder me himself."

Killian lifted the broken vial off the table and held it up to the hint of light streaming through a break in the thick curtains. "This?" His palm landed square on Maddox's chest as the angel tried to lunge for it and Killian lifted it over his head. "You practically begged me to take it from you last night. Which leads me to believe you are not supposed to have it."

"Of course I'm not supposed to have it, you idiot. It's *celestial sand*. No one's supposed to have it. It belongs back on the shores of the Sea of Redemption in the celestial realm. The question you should be asking is 'Why did the witches have it?'"

Before Killian could answer—or remind Maddox that he was, in fact, a witch, something tugged deep inside him, a compulsion he couldn't ignore. "Fuck. Not now." He was being summoned. And he had no choice but to go. The phone fell from his hand, and like back in England, his entire body started to compress, and he met Maddox's terrified gaze. "Don't leave—" he managed as his entire body was sucked into the void, the vial included, and he flew.

"Killian?" Delphine, the New Orleans Coven's High Priestess, sat in a plush, leather chair in an alcove with a curved, leaded glass window, her dark hair highlighted by the gentle rays of sunlight streaming in.

"Bloody hell. I was all of a ten minute walk away, High Priestess. Perhaps a phone call would have been easier than a summoning?" Killian angled his body and tucked the vial into his pocket. He didn't trust Delphine. Not after last night.

Delphine's smooth skin marked her as early forties, but Killian believed her to be much older. It was in the endless depths of her brown eyes, the way she seemed to be able to look right *through* the witches in her charge. And those who weren't.

"Perhaps. Had I been summoning *you*. I was not." She extended her palm. "Hand over the vial, Killian. Do it quickly and I might not have to consign you to the dungeons for the next fifty years."

The dungeons?

Killian dipped his hand into his pocket, upended the vial,

and hoped this *celestial sand* wasn't so fine-grained it would end up on his socks. For fuck's sake, he hadn't put on shoes or even had a chance to button his shirt.

"You mean this?" He held up the empty, broken glass tube. "I found this last night outside the mansion. There was nothing inside. I assumed whoever cursed the lot of us dropped it."

Delphine snapped her fingers, and the vial appeared in her hand. She sniffed it, then held it up to the light. "By the goddess, one grain left. You will answer for this, Killian."

"Answer for what? Your bloody invitation summoned me here—a place I'd hoped never to see again—then you send the one person in the world with more reason to hate me than I do to greet me, subject me to a curse, the effects of which I still have not been able to figure out, and now, you're going to make me 'answer' for a crime I did not commit? That's rich, Delphine. I believed you to be fair and just, if not a bit loony. Clearly, I was wrong."

He was almost desperate enough to lob a spell at the High Priestess, but two burly men stepped from the shadows, slapped iron manacles on his wrists, and locked them behind his back. The iron had to be spelled, because he felt his magic drain, and he glared at Delphine.

"What is the meaning of this?" he snarled.

"Tell me who sent you to steal the celestial sand. And what you know about Thea and the curse." Delphine stood, striding over to him and jabbing at his chest. The new marks flared, and Killian thought he could smell his skin burning.

"I had nothing to do with that bloody vial, I don't know any Thea, and I was cursed along with the lot of you. If you don't believe me, just look." He nodded down at his bare chest. "Do you think I would do *that* to myself? Are you that daft?"

Delphine tugged the shirt away from the marks and narrowed her eyes. "I think it is very possible these are the marks of someone burdened with guilt. Perhaps over stealing that which does not belong to them. Take him to the dungeon and put him on the rack. That should loosen his tongue."

She vanished in front of Killian's eyes, and before he could call her name, one of the men holding him forced his jaw open and shoved a leather bit between his teeth, then tied it behind his head.

"Finally," a sing-song voice said from the corner of the room. "You've been hobbled."

Jezebel.

The two guards muscled him around to face her, and Killian glared, wishing he'd thought to ward the hotel room the previous night.

"Delphine didn't call you here, Killian. Thea did." Jezebel stepped close enough Killian could smell her perfume, something floral and harsh. "It seems she and I had a common enemy in you."

"What did I ever do to her?" His words came out garbled and unintelligible, but Jezebel appeared to understand him. With a laugh, she cupped his cheek, then reared back and slapped him, hard.

"The werewolf you killed? He was a dear friend of hers." After a pause, she shook her head. "Don't look at me like that, murderer. I knew nothing of Thea's plan and I was cursed along with the rest of you. My heart is gone. I feel nothing but anger now. Before, I might have gone easy on you. Not now."

"For every moment you do spend, bound in iron to the end, you will suffer endless pain, find no rest, from sleep abstain. Until you wish to leave this life, for which you'll beg me for the right."

Dark wisps of magic curled from Jezebel's fingers and wound around Killian's throat, all along his chest, and down his arms and legs. Fire and ice warred for dominance inside of him, each burning in their own way, and his knees buckled as tears burned his eyes.

Please, he begged his enemy as the men dragged him from the room and down three flights of stairs to the mansion's basement, past an open crypt, and through another heavy wooden door to the dungeon.

In the third cell, they bound him to a horizontal iron rack, his arms over his head, his ankles locked in heavy manacles. When one of them turned a crank, his entire body stretched, and he groaned as the pain worsened, each breath more difficult than the last.

"The High Priestess will return for you this evening," one of them said as he slammed the iron bars and locked Killian's cell. "If you last that long."

Bound, spelled, and with a pile of celestial sand in the pocket of his trousers, Killian screamed obscenities at them through the gag, but the two of them only laughed as they left him alone.

Fuck. What was he supposed to do now?

CHAPTER SIX

MADDOX

He had to be seeing things. Or...not seeing things. Killian had just vanished before his eyes. With the vial. Where he'd once stood, only his scent lingered. His phone still rattled on the floor where he dropped it.

Maddox scanned the room. Killian's wallet rested on the nightstand. If there were ever a time to pry... Maddox flipped open the billfold and pulled out Killian's driver's license.

"England?" Well, that explained the accent. The very sexy, very addictive accent. As he rifled through the rest of the wallet, he found a couple of credit cards, a handful of bills—British and American money, he thought—and a folded image. Saying a silent apology for the invasion, Maddox spread the picture out on the bed.

Two young men stared back at him from in front of a darkened hearth. One, obviously Killian, and the other, well, he was perfection preserved in technicolor. Long, wavy brown hair, piercing green eyes, a strong jaw. Muscular, with his arm around Killian in a way that was definitely more than friendly. Despite how happy the two looked, when Maddox dragged his fingers over Killian's smiling face, an intense wave of sadness hit him. Regret. Pain.

He couldn't invade Killian's privacy any more than he already had, so he folded up the picture and tucked it back into the man's wallet.

"Don't leave..."

Killian had been clear about his wishes. Not his reasons. And from the look on his face, he hadn't *wanted* to be summoned. Was Maddox in danger if he stayed? He couldn't simply wait around for the witches to come for him. And if they *had* summoned Killian, it wouldn't be long before Killian told them Maddox had stolen the vial.

Maddox glanced down at his shirt on the end of the bed. Bloodied and ripped in several places. His pants were stained with dirt. He couldn't go out like this. Killian was taller and thinner than he was, but perhaps...something in the closet would fit him?

He had to find the witch. And the vial. He prayed the talisman Azrael had given him would still let him back into the celestial realm. He'd already missed his appointed time to return. But he knew one thing for certain. If he did not return with the sand—his immortal life would be over, and he, like his brother, would be banished forever.

~

AFTER A COLD SHOWER TO help shake off the last bits of his broken sleep and injuries, Maddox stood naked in front of the closet. His various bruises and mending bones still pained him, but they'd mostly healed overnight, and after he'd hidden his wings, Maddox found a v-neck t-shirt in deep purple that would stretch enough, he thought, and managed to get it over his head with only a minimal amount of grunting.

A pair of briefs from the dresser were snug, but not uncomfortable. The pants, on the other hand, those were a lost cause. Too tight and too long.

Shaking out his stained white trousers from the previous night, he slid them on, along with his shoes, and tucked Killian's wallet and phone into his back pocket. First stop, somewhere that sold pants. Second? Wherever the fuck Killian had gone.

KILLIAN

Jezebel's magic ate away at his strength. The iron burned his wrists and ankles, and he couldn't move beyond thrashing his head about trying to remove the gag. What in the bloody hell was he supposed to do now? The dungeons were spelled, so even if he could get free from the iron manacles that dampened his power and held him down, he couldn't use his magic.

The gag was bloody painful, though. He rubbed his head harder against the iron and wood rack, trying to loosen the damn thing, and finally, the leather cord slipped, and he was able to push the bit free so it hung around his neck instead.

Just how long was Delphine planning on leaving him down here? He had no phone, no shoes, and no hope of escape. From the rumors over the years, Delphine Perdue didn't believe in barristers or trials. She was judge and jury.

"Delphine!" Raising his voice to a shout, he continued, "Let me out of here! I did nothing wrong."

His curses echoed off the walls, but the High Priestess either wasn't within earshot or didn't give a damn.

"You'll never see daylight again," a woman said from another cell. Her voice was weak, and Killian heard the rattling of chains as she moved.

"Who are you?" He strained to raise his head a fraction, and as he did, searing pain lashed across his chest again and he stifled a groan. Looking down in the dim light, he struggled to breathe as another long, curved black burn mark appeared underneath the first.

Fucking curse.

"I don't remember my name," the woman said. "I only know it was stolen by dark magic. Magic I helped Thea bring into this place."

"Thea? Who the fuck is she?" Killian could barely get the words out. Between the pain of Jezebel's magic and the weakness from the iron, he desperately wanted to pass out, but feared he'd be unable to.

The woman—the witch—coughed, wet and rattling, and then the chains scraped across the stone floor. "She's the reason Delphine will never let you go. The curse...it plays on your deepest fears. Mine was not being remembered. By anyone. Now, I can't be. No one knows my name. Or anything about me, other than what I've done."

"Why does the curse mean I will never get out of here?" Killian stopped fighting his bonds, unable to muster the strength any longer.

"Because I know Delphine's greatest fear." The witch coughed again, and her next words were faint. "She fears admitting her mistakes. Even if you did nothing wrong, she'll still keep you here forever."

"Witch? Witch!" No further noise greeted him. The nameless woman had either passed out or no longer wished to speak to him. With nothing to distract from the constant agony of the spell eating away at him, Killian sank into the pain. The dungeons were cool and damp, and the rack hard. His entire body ached, and he needed food and water.

He floated from memory to memory, Oliver screaming, the stench of burnt werewolf fur, his would-be lover's last breath, the fear as Jezebel and the townspeople came for him.

Every time one of the marks on his chest flared, he snarled and jerked against his bonds, but it was no use. Even at full strength, he'd be unable to escape them. Squinting in the dim light, he managed to croak, "Fuck me," as he glanced down at his shirt. Wherever it had been touching the marks, it had burned, half a dozen arcs and whorls now clearly evident on the light blue material.

What had Delphine said to him? The burns were marks of someone burdened with guilt? Was this his curse? To relive the worst day of his life while trapped in iron and Jeze's spell? Alone and powerless?

Closing his eyes, he called up the memory of Oliver's face, trying to focus on his smile. "I'm so sorry. I was careless. A complete tosser. And you...you were everything I was not."

If this was his fate, he would accept it. He'd done the unforgivable. Killed the one man he was supposed to protect above all others. The first and only man he'd thought he just might...fall in love with.

Despite the burning in his chest, he was so tired, and the iron weakened him every minute it touched his skin. A burst of pure agony washed over him, but it wasn't Oliver's name he screamed...he could utter only one word.

"Maddox!"

CHAPTER SEVEN

MADDOX

In the middle of the menswear dressing room two blocks from the hotel, Maddox's head exploded in pain. Something was very wrong. Not with him. As he sank down on the little bench in the corner and closed his eyes, he saw Killian. Bound to a rack. Writhing in pain. Deep, blackened burns across his chest. Where this morning, Maddox had only seen three or four odd lines marring Killian's sculpted muscles, now, there were more than a dozen.

A wave of dizziness overtook him as he tried to stand, but Maddox fought it off long enough to zip up the new pants, yank off the tags, and thrust a handful of bills at the confused human behind the counter. He'd probably just overpaid by half, but he didn't care. He had to get to Killian.

Maddox lurched down the street with no idea of where he was going. More than once, he pulled out the celestial token, so desperate, he was willing to ask Azrael for help. But after almost an hour, the pain in his head muddling his sense of direction, he felt a pull so strong, it was like someone had tied a string to his heart and yanked on it.

He had to go back to Magnolia House. Maddox tried to stop, but his feet had a mind of their own, and soon, he found himself outside the fence, hiding behind a row of bushes.

A group of three witches exited the mansion, one obviously in charge. She was beautiful. Long, dark hair fell over one shoulder, and she walked with an air of superiority while the other two flanked her.

"How long will you leave him down there, Delphine?" the witch on the left asked.

"Until midnight. If your spell permanently damages him, you will find yourself in the dungeon with him. I have indulged your desires too often, I think, for your own good."

"But my brother—"

"Your brother drained that werewolf's mate. Killian was reckless and wild, but Oliver would have died that night no matter what he'd done, witch. Now focus. We have to get into Killian's hotel room. Perhaps the sand is there."

Maddox took off around the corner as the witches exited the gate. A few moments later, he approached the same door he'd used the previous night. Only this time, it hung open.

The kitchen was deserted. Broken glasses littered the floor and his shoes made odd sucking sounds as he crept towards the hall.

The whole manor felt...wrong somehow. As if whatever had happened the night before had left it stripped bare. Maddox knew little of curses and even less about the one leveled the previous night, but he had vague memories of a large crowd running and screaming all around him as he'd fled.

Sending a quick burst of his celestial power to swirl around him, cloaking him to all but those specifically searching for him, he made his way down the same grand hallway as the night before. Velvet wraps, coats, purses, and the occasional shoe were strewn about the rooms.

The pull deep in his chest took him down the stairs to the basement, past the crypt—which was shuttered tightly once more—and to another, smaller and plainer door. This one had no handle. Only a thick deadbolt. It was not guarded by magic. Not that he could sense. But his power would not work against human inventions. Only the spiritual.

Pulling out Killian's phone, Maddox dialed the number Sin had made him memorize years ago when his brother had first taken up residence on earth.

"Who is this?" Sin said, his voice booming in the deathly quiet cavern.

Mad jabbed the volume button several times, then whispered, "It's Mad. I don't have a lot of time. But I'm in this realm, and I need your help."

"Mad? Where are you? I'll come to you—"

"No. Don't. Trust me, Sin. This is something I have to do on my own. Mostly. In your work with that human law enforcement agency...did you ever learn how to pick a lock?"

TEN MINUTES LATER, after much swearing and frustration on both of their parts, the lock tumblers clicked, and the door creaked open. "I have to go, brother. Please do not try to find me. There is magic at work here. A curse. And we don't know what its effects will be."

"Maddox, wait." Sinclair's plea was so full of emotion,

Maddox stopped just inside the door. "You're in New Orleans, aren't you?"

"H-how did you know?"

"There are rumors everywhere. Witches going insane. Dark magic taking over. If you get into trouble, there's a vampire I know. Her name is Mist, and she can be found at the House of Voodoo every night after sunset. Tell her I sent you."

"Mist. Thank you, Sin. I...I hope I get to see you again." Before his brother could protest, Maddox ended the call and shut off the phone. The last thing he needed was the damn thing ringing and alerting someone to his presence.

Creeping down the stairs, he caught the scent of iron heavy in the air. Also, a hint of Killian. He was here. A dozen cells lined a long hallway, and at the third one, he stopped, horror stirring in his chest.

Killian lay on his back, his breathing labored. His unbuttoned shirt was singed in a dozen locations, and his skin was almost bone-white. "N-no," he moaned as he shook his head —the only movement he seemed to be capable of bound as he was. "Forgive...me."

"Killian?" Maddox pulled out the hairpins he'd found in one of the ballrooms upstairs and went to work on the cell door's heavy lock. His witch didn't answer, and another black circle burned his flesh just over his heart. The agonized cry tore Mad apart, and he bit his lip as he tried to concentrate on the tumblers and tune out Killian's suffering.

He'd always been a quick study, and as soon as he had the door open, he cupped the witch's cheek. "Killian, it's Mad. Open your eyes."

With a grunt of surprise, Killian jerked, and his blue-gray eyes struggled to focus. "Brilliant," he rasped. "I'm hallucinating."

"No, you're not." Maddox prayed he still had some of his angelic strength left as he grabbed the small padlocks securing the ankle fetters. With a quick snap, they broke off in his hands, and he freed Killian's legs. The wrist cuffs...those he had to pick, and when he was done, he took Killian's arm. "Come on. We have to get out of here."

Shaking his head and blinking hard, Killian let out a shuddering breath. "The spell. It's gone." His confused gaze went to his wrists, and he turned his hands over, squinting at the chafing from the metal cuffs. "Maddox? I'm not dreaming?"

"No. But even if you were, dream-you needs to come with me. Right now. Can you walk?"

"If you help me." Killian draped his arm around Maddox's shoulders and warmth seeped into Mad's every pore. He *needed* Killian. Needed to hold him and make sure he was going to be okay.

"I've got you, baby," Maddox said quietly, then cringed. Why had he called Killian that? At least the witch didn't notice—or didn't care.

"There's another witch here." Killian's voice was faint, even right in his ear.

"I don't know how long we have before someone—" A cold draft made Maddox shiver, and he checked all around them to make sure they were still alone.

"I have to see her." Killian tugged him down to the far end of the dungeon and peered into the last cell on the right. "Witch. Witch!"

A woman lay on the floor next to the door, her skin gray. Killian sank down to his knees and reached his free hand through the bars to touch her neck before toppling over into Maddox's legs. "Fuck. She's dead."

"Can we get out of here now?" Maddox asked. "Something's...coming. Something dark. I can feel it."

He practically hauled Killian against his chest as he wrapped an arm around the witch's waist to support him. Before they could take a step, Killian turned, reached up, and cupped the back of Maddox's neck. Digging his other hand into his pocket, he came away with a small pile of celestial sand.

"Truth, Maddox. Did you come here for me or for the sand?"

Mad stared down at the grains glittering in Killian's palm, closed the man's fingers over the dust, and leaned in, pressing his lips to Killian's jaw. "For you."

KILLIAN

He didn't know why he'd asked the angel about his intentions. It shouldn't have mattered. Killian could have died in the dungeon—or gone insane from Jezebel's torture—and now he was held against a fighter's body, Maddox's warmth strengthening him with each step, and almost back above ground.

The sand weighed him down, tethered him to this world of magic he wanted no part of after Delphine's betrayal. He thought about just letting it go, but then he'd be leaving it in the one place Maddox didn't want it to be, and he couldn't disappoint the man that way. Not after the feel of Maddox's lips on his skin.

As they rounded a corner and found themselves in the grand ballroom, Maddox froze, then pointed to one of the room's three exits. *"Someone's coming,"* he mouthed and pulled Killian towards another door.

A blast of magic hit Killian square in the back, and his body stopped listening to his commands. He slumped in Maddox's arms, barely managing to grunt, "I'm...sorry. Take the sand. Leave me."

"Killian Wade! You will burn for this," Jezebel shouted as she raced for them. But Maddox just threw Killian's paralyzed body over his shoulder and took off at a run. They burst through the mansion's front doors, and Maddox ducked down an alley, around three other buildings, and then cut through a narrow side street, evading the occasional blasts of magic Jezebel hurled their way.

Even with Killian's extra weight, Maddox was faster, and when they could no longer hear Jezebel's heels clicking on the sidewalks, Maddox eased Killian to his feet and propped him up against the side of a building.

"Killian, baby, listen to me. I need you to tell me how to break this spell."

He couldn't speak. Every muscle in his body was locked tight, even his hand, where, in his fist, the celestial grains were still held securely.

Maddox searched his face, then pulled him closer and kissed him. Not a gentle brush to his cheek, but a kiss that consumed him. When Maddox's tongue darted out to trace the seam of Killian's lips, the marks across his chest flared to life, but this time, the searing agony didn't follow. Instead, they were warm, comforting, and seemed to reach deep into his soul.

The spell loosened, and Killian opened for the angel, each fighting for dominance as Maddox pressed him harder to the wall. The thick, hard rod against Killian's thigh set off his own arousal, and as his dick responded in kind, the last vestiges of the spell shattered.

"Maddox," Killian whispered. "You..."

"Can you stand?" the angel demanded.

Nodding, Killian took a step back, suddenly worried he'd done something to offend Maddox. But in the next second, Mad stripped off his shirt and draped it over his shoulder. "You're not going to like this. Hold on. Arms around my neck, legs at my waist. And Killian? Once we're airborne, start dropping the sand. Scatter it to the winds. If we can't keep it safe, then we'll make sure no one has it."

"I don't understand—" Despite the absence of Jezebel's magic, Killian's mind was still addled. The sun was starting to set. He'd passed at least six hours in the dungeon, the torturous spell denying him any respite and the iron leaching the magic from his body.

But he fell silent as Maddox's wings burst forth, pure white, more than seven feet across, and covered with lush feathers.

"We're going to fly, Killian. It's the only way we can get out of here safely."

Maddox grabbed the backs of Killian's thighs and hefted him so Killian could wind his arms around Maddox's neck. Hooking one foot over the other behind the angel's back, he relished their closeness, even as his stomach pitched at the thought of flying.

"Do you trust me, Killian?" Maddox asked, holding his gaze, emotion churning in his dark brown eyes.

Killian kissed him back, hard and fast. "Yes. With my life."

A breeze ruffled Killian's hair as Maddox's wings flapped once, twice, and then...they were off the ground, Killian staring up at the cloudy sky as Maddox carried him off somewhere he hoped they'd both be safe.

CHAPTER EIGHT

MADDOX

Having Killian's arms around him settled Maddox in a way he wasn't sure he'd ever felt before. Like he was home. They flew over the city, and when Killian let go of the celestial sand, Maddox hoped to all that was good in his life that Azrael would forgive him. Better to ensure it was destroyed than to let it fall into the wrong hands.

"Where do we go?" Maddox asked, his lips close to Killian's ear.

"I don't know this city." Killian's voice was weaker than it had been only a few minutes ago, and his grip around Maddox's neck loosened slightly. "Somewhere...I can rest. Hotel. No good to you like this."

"Hang on, Killian. Don't let go. Please." Maddox's left wing was starting to tire and ache, and he didn't think he could fly them much farther. Digging deep inside for any shred of power he had left, he tried to cloak them both as he dove towards a side street on the outskirts of the city.

As soon as they landed, Killian slumped in his hold. A delicious scent—sweet and rich and *fried*—wafted over them, and Killian groaned. "Food. I'm knackered. Don't suppose you...brought my wallet?"

Maddox flushed, the heat crawling up his cheeks. "Um, I might have spent some of your money on these pants."

A weak smile curved Killian's full lips. "Cursing *and* stealing? Angels are nothing like I imagined."

"I'll pay you back," Maddox rushed to assure him. "I just—"

"No." Brushing a shaking hand down Maddox's hip, Killian whispered, "I'm winding you up, mate. Joking."

"At a time like this? You can barely stand." Maddox hated the anger in his voice, but he was so worried about his witch he couldn't think straight.

"Trying to get you to smile." With a sigh, Killian glanced around them. The side street was empty, and a few doors down, a handful of tables and chairs were arranged outside a little cafe. "Are there any bills left?"

Opening the wallet, Maddox pulled out three twenty-dollar-bills. "I've never paid for anything before. The last time I was in this realm, my brother took care of everything."

Sliding a single twenty free from the rest, Killian pressed it into Maddox's palm. "This should be enough for some sweets. Beignets. Six of them. And strong tea. Earl Gray or Oolong."

"Beignets and tea? That will be enough?" Maddox crushed the bill in his fist, and the idea of leaving Killian out here, exposed, didn't sit well with him.

"Enough for now. I can't bloody think straight." The admission cost Killian, the price a dulling of his eyes and a hollow tinge to his tone. "I'm no good to you like this, Maddox."

"I need you to promise me something," Maddox said as he helped Killian to the chairs and eased him down. "You will keep watch while I am inside. I almost lost you at Magnolia House. I won't risk that again."

Killian pulled him closer. His lips slanted over Maddox's, and their connection flared, the heat of it driving the ache from his wings and the slight throbbing from around his temples. "I don't know what it is about you, Mad," Killian whispered when they finally parted, "but every time I kiss you, I feel…stronger."

Maddox very much wanted to hear Killian use his nickname again. And spend hours kissing him, just to see how much stronger Killian could get. But then the witch shuddered, and Maddox pushed himself up. "We're going to test that more…after we eat."

Killian had his head in his hands when Maddox returned with a tray of beignets and tea, and it wasn't until he touched the witch that he let himself breathe. "What was that spell that vile woman used on you?"

A few drops of tea sloshed over the edge of the mug as Killian took a tentative sip. "That was Jezebel. She fancies locking spells. In the dungeon, she forced me to relive my greatest pain over and over again. Upstairs, before we escaped, she quite literally turned my body into a prison. I couldn't breathe or move, and what little I had of my own magic…she used against me."

"I do not like this Jezebel. Her name suits her." Maddox bit into one of the beignets. The fried pillow covered in powdered sugar made him moan, and he took a moment to savor the treat. "I forgot how good earthen realm food is."

Killian laughed, the sound weak, but at the same time, still rich. "You surprise me, Maddox. Constantly."

"Is that a good thing?"

Reaching across the table, Killian brushed his thumb across Maddox's lips and came away with a lump of powdered sugar. And then did the sexiest thing Maddox had ever seen. He licked the sugar off his own thumb with a smile.

"Yes. It is."

Grateful for the table hiding his growing erection, Maddox tore into another beignet, focusing on the fried dough so he could have a moment to breathe. Or try to. Magic. Danger. Jezebel. Forcing his thoughts back to the present, he swallowed hard. "Why does Jezebel hate you so?"

The heavy sigh should have warned Maddox to leave it well enough alone, but he couldn't. Not when he suspected he was falling for the witch.

"Killian? Tell me."

"I killed her brother."

Maddox jerked up, nearly knocking over his chair in the process. "You...what?"

The horror on Killian's face was enough to make Maddox's heart feel like someone was squeezing it in a vise grip. When the witch spoke again, his voice was so full of emotion, Maddox had to strain to hear the words.

"We grew up together. The three of us. Oliver and Jezebel are—were—witches too. Until Oliver was attacked by a vampire when he was twenty. Though I suppose he was still a witch, just one who couldn't go out in the light of day." Killian ran a hand through his hair, and a faraway look settled in his eyes. "We spent every night together, lived just a few kilometers from one another. And I...cared for him. He was the first man I ever kissed." Killian's voice lowered even further. "And the last. Before you."

Shock kept Maddox from saying anything as Killian pushed his plate away and scowled into his tea. "I'm a bloody pisser of a witch, Maddox. Never could get a handle on my magic. My High Priestess—the leader of my coven—swears it's because I'm too powerful. But I know that's not the truth. I'm simply rubbish at it."

As the silence spread between them, Maddox used his gifts to reach out and sense Killian's emotions. So many churned within the depths of his soul. Regret, shame, sorrow, loss, grief...

Killian met Maddox's gaze, and desperation surged over their connection. An intense need to find acceptance lingered in his eyes, and Maddox reached across the table for Killian's hand. "Tell me. All of it," he said quietly as he linked their fingers.

But in the next moment, Killian groaned, his free hand clawing at his chest. "The curse...it's getting stronger," he whispered as he loosed the top two buttons of his shirt. His brand, the one Maddox now recognized as his very own wings, was glowing red hot, and Killian wavered in his seat, finally collapsing back and panting through the pain.

"We need to get you somewhere you can rest," Maddox said as he leapt up and then draped Killian's arm over his shoulders. Now, the only thing he saw in Killian's eyes was sorrow.

CHAPTER NINE

KILLIAN

He should have kept his mouth shut. It had to have been the spell. It addled his mind. Made it hard to think. Or hell, maybe the curse. After all, he'd kissed *an angel*. More than once. And he'd wanted to do it again.

Until he'd admitted his darkest secret. Now, as Maddox helped him down the street, he doubted he'd ever have the chance to be this close to the angel again once they got where they were going. Maddox would leave, and Killian... he'd have to figure this curse shite out on his own.

"We should find a boarding house. Somewhere with only a few rooms," Killian said as they wove their way through the few people out and about on the edges of the city. "They might not computerize records. And I need to make some calls."

Maddox nodded and then handed Killian his phone, but

didn't otherwise speak. He looked shell-shocked, and Killian tried to hold on to the spark of connection they'd had ever since he'd rescued the angel outside the mansion, but the pain in his chest, his exhaustion, and the terrible look on Maddox's face warned him that was folly.

Two blocks away, now acutely aware he wasn't wearing any shoes, Killian spied a row house with a "Rooms for Rent Nightly" sign in the window. A place like this might not run his credit card right away. Not if he looked...normal. Which, of course, he didn't. Fuck. He was going to have to use his magic.

"I need you to stand back," he said as he pulled his arm away from Maddox's strong shoulders and prayed his legs would hold him. "This could be dangerous. For both of us. But we can't get rooms with me looking like a vagrant."

Maddox stepped back, though uncertainty lingered in his brown eyes. Fuck, Killian wanted to reassure him, but he was too scared he'd knock down the entire building unintentionally. Ducking into an alley and turning away, he almost convinced himself it was better to face reality now. He and Maddox had no future together. They were simply two people in the right place at the right time to help one another. And that time would soon be over.

Trying desperately to center himself, Killian reached for his magic. It was always there, just under his skin, but now, without the dampening cuff, it felt wild. Untamable. And he feared it—more than he feared anything. Including his own death.

"From prying eyes, now do hide, all that frightens and derides. Those who look will only see exactly what I wish to be."

The spell crackled over his skin, and the new brand under his shirt flared again, red hot, then cooled as the charm took hold. Behind him, Maddox gasped.

"It worked, then?" Killian asked as he turned back to the angel.

"You're wearing a suit. Boots. The blood stains are gone. As is your stubble. You look...perfect." The last word escaped almost on a sigh, and Killian longed to take the man in his arms and apologize for everything. But he couldn't hold the charm for long, so instead, he pushed past Maddox and headed for the row house.

"Come on. I'll get us a couple of rooms. We're businessmen in town for a conference." He kept his voice level, but inside, his heart wanted to crack into pieces.

Until Maddox threaded his arm through his. "No. One room. You can be the businessman. I'm just tagging along for a vacation with you."

"Maddox—"

"Not here." The angel opened the front door and gestured for Killian to enter. "The rest of this conversation requires privacy. And maybe alcohol."

Killian shook his head as he climbed the three steps up into a small lobby. "You are a very bad angel."

"You have no idea."

A WHITE-HAIRED GENTLEMAN named Frank at the check-in desk took Killian's credit card and ran it through an old-fashioned carbon-copy machine. "Just for incidentals, y'hear? Bill's due when you check out."

At least something was going right for him. Killian breathed a sigh of relief and leaned an elbow on the counter. "I don't suppose there are any stores in the area that deliver? Some cock-up with the airline sent our baggage to New York City, and we won't have it back for two days."

Frank huffed. "Airlines don't give a crap about service these days, do they? Paul's Menswear will fix you up. You call them in the morning and tell them Frank sent you." He looked them up and down. "Actually, here." He slid a pad of paper and a pen across the counter. "Write down your sizes and what you need. You've probably been traveling all night and day, yeah? I'll call them first thing in the morning."

Killian offered the man a weary smile. "You're a proper gentleman, Frank. Have them charge everything to the same card as the room." After scribbling a short list for the both of them, he accepted the key from Frank and thanked the man.

Before he could say a word, Maddox snatched the key from his hand and threaded his arm through Killian's. "Come on, love. The trip was brutal. We need to sleep."

Killian's cheeks heated, and he offered Frank a shrug as Maddox led him up the stairs and down the hall to their room. *Their room.*

As soon as Maddox flicked the lock behind them, Killian dropped the charm. His feet ached, and the brand across his chest was a constant dull burn. Stripping off his filthy socks and tossing them in the trash, he went directly into the bathroom. "I need a shower. Take the bed. Get some rest," he said as he shut the door.

A wispy tendril of smoke curled up from Killian's shirt, and he swore and yanked off the burnt, stained, and torn material. In the bathroom mirror, he stared in wonder at the markings across his chest. No longer simply lines and whorls, they'd taken shape—a shape Killian recognized. Angel wings.

Killian traced shaking fingers over the design. They were nearly complete. Thick lines arced from his sternum all the way along his collarbones. The feathers bore reddish hues, and as he inhaled deeply, they almost seemed to move—just as Maddox's feathers had done when he'd extended his wings.

Fuck. He understood now. Maddox was his curse. The Divine had given him a second chance, but Thea had taken it from him—from both of them. Because there was no way Maddox would ever accept him. Not after what he'd done. And with how badly Delphine wanted what Maddox had stolen, the angel's life—his earthen life—was forfeit.

He had to convince Maddox to go back to the celestial realm. It was the only place he'd be safe.

Turning on the shower, Killian stripped, tossing all of his clothes into the trash. As worried as he was about Delphine and Jezebel tracking them down, he needed a few minutes to think. To figure out how to drive Maddox away without destroying the angel—or himself—in the process. The hot water ran down his back, easing the tension in his muscles, and for a moment, he let himself remember kissing Maddox. How good he'd felt held in the angel's embrace as they'd flown over the city.

He'd been terrified. Contrary to all the stories that involved brooms, most witches didn't actually fly. But with Mad...the terror had quickly faded.

"Killian." Maddox stepped into the shower, wrapping his strong arms around Killian's waist from behind.

"Don't."

"Don't what?" The angel's cock pressed against Killian's arse, and his hands traveled up to the wings branded across his chest. "Don't touch you? Don't comfort you?"

"None of it." Killian pulled away, wiping the water off his forehead and slicking back his hair. "I don't deserve—"

"What do you know about angels, Killian?" Maddox turned him, cupped his cheeks, and pressed a gentle kiss to his lips.

"Nothing, it seems."

A bottle of body wash sat on a little shelf in the corner, and Maddox spilled some into his hands, then started massaging Killian's shoulders and back. "I'm a lesser angel. All of us are, other than the archangels. I don't have power over life and death. I can't cure disease, can't take away pain."

His strong fingers worked a particularly tight knot at the base of Killian's neck, and Killian groaned. "I beg to differ. You're doing a bloody good job of that at the moment."

Maddox's chuckle settled Killian in a way he hadn't known he needed, and he relaxed as the angel's hands traveled lower, down, over his ribs, to his obliques, carefully avoiding the now sodden bandage on his side.

"We can fly, of course. Those of us who have earned our wings. We have a small bit of glamour. You might call it...a perception filter of sorts. It's what allowed me to sneak into Magnolia House without being seen."

Now, his fingers cupped Killian's arse, and his voice lowered as he pressed closer. "We have one more ability."

"If you're going to tell me you have a magical willy, be prepared to prove it." Killian's own cock stood at attention, and he ached to bury himself deep inside the angel, but he didn't deserve even this much closeness, let alone more.

"Well, to be honest, I don't know. I've never..."

"Never?" Killian angled his head to catch Maddox's gaze over his shoulder. "You're...beyond fit."

"Fit?"

Killian almost laughed. "Sorry. It's a phrase where I come from. Means...hot. Handsome. Fuckable."

"Oh." Maddox curled one arm around Killian's waist and rested his cheek on Killian's shoulder. "Fit. I like that."

Get over yourself, Killian. Of course he's a virgin. He's a bloody angel. And he's certainly not going to come down to earth to fuck you.

"I want you, Killian," Maddox whispered in his ear. "That last ability? We can sense emotions. Human emotions. Joy, sorrow, regret, fear...all of them. Including need. And arousal."

Thick fingers wrapped around Killian's cock, and Maddox angled them so the water sluiced down their joined bodies, providing just enough lubrication for him to start stroking slowly, up and down Killian's shaft. He rubbed his thumb over the crown, and Killian shuddered.

"I killed—"

"I know, baby. And you need to tell me all of it. But I used my gifts to sense your feelings at the cafe, and I know...I know you're a good person. One who'd never kill on purpose. It was an accident, yes? You lost control of your magic?"

He was still gripping Killian's arousal, his movements slow and controlled, and Killian groaned, "Yes."

With his free hand, Maddox traced the lines across Killian's chest. "I may not be able to work miracles, but I know a sign when I see one. *This* is a sign. A beautiful, perfect sign." Quickening his strokes, Maddox closed his teeth over the shell of Killian's ear, and pleasure shot through him, all the way down to his balls.

"I won't last," Killian grunted as Maddox gripped harder, using his thumb along the pulsing vein on the underside of Killian's cock. A drop of pre-cum escaped his slit, and Maddox inhaled deeply. Against Killian's arse, the angel's dick throbbed, hot and thick, and shite. He'd never been much for playing the bottom, but fuck if he didn't want the angel inside of him.

"Let go, baby. Just...let go," Maddox urged, and when he

started kissing down Killian's neck, the pleasure overtook him.

With a strangled moan, Killian did as his angel asked, and his seed painted the shower wall, coating Maddox's hand, the scent mixing with the soap and filling the steamy air.

Fuck. Killian needed more, but as he collapsed against Maddox's strong chest, his exhaustion caught up with him, and he slumped in the angel's embrace.

"Shhh, Killian. Let me take care of you now."

A RHYTHMIC POUNDING *roused him from sleep, and Killian rolled over, the sheets whispering over his skin. He could sense his angel. Close by. Happy. Fulfilled.*

Wrapping himself in his flannel robe, Killian trudged out to their kitchen. He could still smell Maddox all over him. The scent of their lovemaking. Of home.

"What are you doing, angel?" he asked as he leaned against the door jamb. Maddox brought an axe down onto a fat log, splitting it into two pieces.

"Keeping us warm," Mad replied with a smile as he swiped a hand across his brow. His dark brown hair was damp, and the muscles of his back glistened from the hard work.

"I have all sorts of ways we can accomplish that particular task." Killian loosened the belt of his robe to show Maddox his growing arousal.

"Stop that." Maddox hefted the axe again, then looked over his shoulder to give Killian a wink. "At least until I'm done here."

"We have enough firewood for the winter," Killian said. "But it's been hours since I had you. Come inside. I'll draw a bath."

"Give me ten minutes, love. I like this work. It feels...good."

Killian couldn't ignore the happiness in his angel's voice. Every day, Maddox surprised him.

Jerking awake, Killian rolled over to find Maddox in the bed next to him. The angel had helped him wash his hair, wrapped him in a fluffy robe, and tucked him in. And now, he slept soundly, the bruises on his torso nearly gone, and his handsome face relaxed.

The dream had felt so real. The two of them, living together, *being* together. Like they were meant to find one another. Killian stared down at the brand on his chest. The angel wings were nearly complete, and when he touched them, they glowed with a subtle warmth. Wrapping his arms around Maddox, Killian closed his eyes and let sleep take him.

CHAPTER TEN

MADDOX

A knock at the door made Maddox jump and his heart stick in his throat. The clock on the bedside table read a little after ten in the morning, and as he scrambled out of bed and shrugged into his robe, his stomach rumbled loudly.

Checking the peep hole, he blew out a breath. Frank stood in the hall, holding several bags with *Paul's Menswear* printed across them in big, golden letters.

"Here you go, son," Frank said as he handed over the bags. "Everything you ordered. You need anything else?"

"Food," Maddox said. "I can go out and get it, but I don't know the area."

"Nonsense." Frank nodded towards Killian, tucked under the blankets. "Truth be told, you're the only guests today. The only guests I've had all week. You want pastries? Something more substantial? You ever had a shrimp po' boy?"

Maddox had no idea what that was, but he thought they

needed more than just sweets. He offered Frank a smile. "No, sir. This is our first time in New Orleans."

"Then if you can wait a little over an hour, I can hit up the best place for 'em in the French Quarter." After patting Maddox on the shoulder, Frank shut the door, and Mad sighed. Maybe he should rest. Curl up with Killian and let the witch know he wasn't going anywhere.

Or... Retrieving Killian's phone from the bathroom counter, he slipped the room key into his pocket and stepped out into the hall to call his brother. Sin would know what to do, and maybe...if he had a plan by the time Killian woke up, he'd be able to convince the witch to stay with him. For good.

"MAD, THANK FUCK," Sin said as soon as he picked up the phone. "Don't do that to me again."

"I'm sorry. But I had...something important to take care of." Maddox rested his back against the wall and sank down onto his ass. "I'm in trouble, Sinclair."

"No shit. You're in New Orleans. Are you going to see Mist tonight?"

"Probably. I haven't gotten that far yet. Until Killian can—"

"Killian?" Sin's voice rose slightly. "Mad? Who's Killian?"

Maddox told his brother everything. The bargain he'd made with Azrael. How the curse had blinded him, sent him into the path of an oncoming car. Killian saving his life. How he was falling for the handsome, tortured witch. And how they'd scattered the celestial sand to the winds.

"I failed, Sin. I wanted to help you. To bring you back to the celestial realm. What good is an angel who can't save his own brother?"

"Maddox, you are *not* to live your life for *me*. I know you wish to help me atone for my mistakes. But I was the one who fell prey to La Fiura. I let her control me, use me in the most vile of ways, and kill...so many people." Sin's voice cracked, and he cleared his throat. "Atoning for my crimes... that is something only I can do, brother."

"But Sin, I don't want to return to the celestial realm without you." Maddox thunked his head against the wall and stared up at the ceiling.

Over the line, a sigh carried. "Brother, I don't think you want to return to the celestial realm at all."

Maddox closed his eyes. "There's nothing *there* for me. Without you, without..."

Killian.

"Mad, no one can live their life for another. That isn't truly *living*. You're half human. You were born of two worlds. As was I. And at some point, you must make a choice. The human world, or the celestial one." Someone knocked at Sinclair's door, and he cursed under his breath. "I have to go, Mad. But please...whatever you do...do it for yourself."

When he returned to the room, Killian was still asleep, and seeing the man's face relaxed did something to Mad's insides he liked very much. Stripping off his robe, he climbed into bed and draped his arm over Killian's waist. Sleep wouldn't come, though. He could only think back over his very long celestial life. If he stayed on earth, would he retain his immortality? He could definitely be hurt. His various injuries were mostly healed, but when he moved, he still felt the dull ache in his arm and wing.

Bruises decorated his torso, fading now into yellow and deep purple. His fingers ghosted over the bandage on Killian's side, and he wished he had Raphael's unique gift of healing.

"Do that again," Killian murmured, his voice thick with sleep.

"This?" Mad skimmed a light touch over Killian's ribs. "Why?"

With a quiet grunt, Killian rolled over, and his erection tented the sheets. "You have to ask?"

"Killian, you need to rest." Cupping Killian's cheek, Maddox brushed his lips to his, and suddenly, neither one of them were tired. Killian's fingers threaded through Maddox's hair, pulling him closer and kissing him so thoroughly, Maddox found himself panting when the witch finally pulled away.

"I need you. Need...*this*." Killian linked his fingers with Maddox's. "I don't know why."

"I do." Maddox leaned in, tracing Killian's new brand with his lips and tongue. The witch shuddered under him, thrusting his hips against Mad. "We were meant to find one another."

"This curse..." Killian's voice shook, and he nudged Maddox's chin to get him to look up. "I killed a man. One I cared for. Deeply."

The shimmer in Killian's blue-gray eyes nearly broke him, and Maddox pulled him into his arms. "Tell me. All of it."

They huddled under the blankets, Killian's head on his shoulder. "Oliver was Jezebel's brother. He was turned into a vampire when we were twenty. But he vowed he would not let that come between us."

"You were intimate?" A wave of jealousy rolled along Maddox's spine, and he forced it away. This Oliver was dead and gone, and Killian needed his support now.

"No. We were going on holiday. I think...we'd talked about making it our first time." Swiping at his eyes, Killian turned over, his back to Maddox's chest. "Oliver's sire was reckless. He failed to teach him how to feed without killing. Ollie learned, but not until he'd killed three men by accident. One...he was a werewolf. Another member of the pack came after him."

Killian took a deep breath, and his words started to come faster and faster. "I heard him scream. My home was only two kilometers away, but by the time I arrived, the werewolf had bitten off Oliver's hand and cracked his skull. He was about to charge him with a silver dagger. My spell...I used my magic to shove Oliver out of his path, but I had no control. He landed on a fence post." A single sob escaped Killian's lips, and Maddox tightened his hold on his witch. "I tried to heal him, but I failed. He died in my arms."

"It was an accident. A mistake."

"How can you say that? You're an angel." Killian pushed out of his arms and got to his feet, pacing the room. "How can you be okay with my taking a life? Two, technically, since the werewolf died as well."

"My brother is the best man I have ever known," Maddox said as he twisted the blanket between his fingers. "But he fell under the thrall of one of the worst demons to ever walk the earthen realm or any other. He had no choice in what he did. Yet, he carries the guilt like a mountain on his shoulders. He's why I came to retrieve the sand in the first place. His crimes...they are so legion, he may never earn his way back to the celestial realm. I tried to bargain with the Angel of Death for his soul."

"Bargains have a way of cocking up everything," Killian murmured.

Maddox threw back the blankets and caught Killian's hand to stop his restless movements. "No one is without fault, Killian. Not even angels."

Acutely aware the two of them were only inches apart and completely naked, Maddox appreciated Killian's lithe, toned body. His abs flexed as he tried to take a step back, but Maddox wouldn't let him.

"I want you. I want to taste you. To feel you inside me. Because you're *fit*," Maddox said, using Killian's word. "But also because you have a good heart, a quick mind. You saved my life, knowing nothing about what I'd done, and you did not betray me even when you were being tortured. *That* is a good man."

Silence stretched between them, and Maddox reached out with his gifts to sense Killian's emotions.

Shame. But also desire. He was about to reach for his witch when Killian dropped to his knees.

"Killian," Maddox said, "what are you...?"

And then Killian's lips were around Maddox's cock, and the heat of his mouth, the way his tongue stroked along his shaft made his entire body come alive. Bracing a hand on the wall, Maddox struggled not to groan, but when Killian hummed just as he took Maddox deeper, he lost the battle. He'd never felt like this before. The way his entire body was one tight string, the heaviness in his balls, and how his soul intertwined with Killian's as the witch held his gaze.

"Killian...I can't...hold on—" Maddox threaded his fingers through Killian's hair, angling his head just slightly. The movement let Killian hollow out his cheeks and suck hard, and Maddox's entire body bucked, the pleasure shooting all the way down to his toes.

The witch—*his* witch—swallowed his seed, and the brand across Killian's chest started to glow. His dick pulsed again and again until he had nothing left to give, and Killian carefully drew his lips over Maddox's crown, then sank down onto his ass.

"Maddox, I..."

"Shh, baby." Maddox sank down next to him and took Killian into his arms, and when they kissed, Killian's taste—the taste of Mad's own release mixing with the deliciousness that *was* Killian—ratcheted his arousal. "I want more. I want all of you."

KILLIAN

His angel held his gaze as Killian pulled him up onto the bed. "I don't know what to do," Mad said. "I've never..."

"Just trust me." Guiding him back onto the pillows, Killian covered Maddox's body with his, the heat between them in such stark contrast to the air conditioning blowing through the room.

With gentle caresses and desperate kisses, Killian explored Maddox's body. Muscles that looked to be sculpted by the Divine. Dusky skin, full lips, a six-pack with a sprinkling of hair below leading to a thick, hard cock with a drop of pre-cum glistening on the tip.

"Ready for another go, angel?"

He didn't give Maddox the chance to speak. Instead, he brushed his thumb over Maddox's lips and hoped he'd take the bait. When the man's tongue darted out, Killian groaned. "Fuck me."

"No. Fuck me," Maddox said around Killian's thumb.

In the years since he'd lost Oliver, Killian had only dated three times. Two humans and one witch, a man named Dex. But though he'd slaked his need—and that of his lovers—he'd never felt anything like he felt for Maddox.

Killian tried to hold back, but his dick throbbed, and he

didn't think he'd last much longer. Leaning over to grab his billfold, he rifled through the contents until he found the packet of lube and condom he'd found in his toiletry kit at the Monarch Hotel.

"Trust me, Mad." Squirting a small amount of lube into his hand, he fisted his cock with Maddox watching him, eyes wide. "If this is too much, any of it, just tell me."

After Maddox nodded, Killian lifted his lover's legs, wrapping them around his waist and notching his dick between the hard globes of Mad's arse. With his hand braced on the headboard, he started to move his hips, savoring how the angel's glutes tensed as he slid between Maddox's cheeks and over his hole.

Claiming his lips, Killian thrust his tongue along Mad's, determined to show the man exactly how much he wanted him.

"Please, Killian," Mad whispered. "I feel so...empty."

"Oh, that won't be a problem for long." Pulling back slightly, Killian reached down and ghosted his finger around Mad's tight hole, and the angel whimpered. "Like that, do you?"

Another nod, and Killian added a little pressure. "Relax, angel. Let me in."

Working his index finger slowly, he pushed past the ring of muscle, swallowing Mad's moan as he kissed those full lips again and again. Shite. Even finger-fucking the man was the hottest thing he'd ever done, and by the time he added a second finger, then, eventually, a third, Maddox was panting and begging with every breath.

If he trusted his magic more, he'd have used it to don the condom and avoid losing even a second of their close contact, but this time...their first...had to be perfect, and he wouldn't risk it.

His crown nudged Maddox's newly stretched hole, and he held Mad's gaze. "You are perfect, angel. Your body, your mind, your heart..." With another kiss, Killian pushed in, slowly, waiting for Maddox's body to accept him.

Gasps, followed by a strangled sob accompanied his dick sliding past the tight ring, and then the most delicious pressure he'd ever felt surrounded him.

"Okay, baby?" Killian asked, keeping his hips perfectly still.

"Uh huh." Mad's fingers dug into his arse, sending him balls-deep in a single motion. "Make...me...yours, Killian."

"Mine," Killian growled as he pulled back and then surged forward. They found their rhythm, Killian balancing on one elbow, Mad's legs wrapped around him. With his free hand, he grabbed Maddox's dick and started working up and down the shaft, and the angel cried out.

"Come with me, baby," Killian whispered as he scored his teeth over the angel's ear and thrust as deeply as he could. He couldn't hold on any longer, and when they fell over the edge, they did it together.

CHAPTER ELEVEN

MADDOX

*S*till hazy from the intensity of coupling with his witch, Maddox barely noticed the knock at the door, or Killian accepting the sandwiches from Frank and coming back to bed.

"Are you all right?" Killian asked as he shed his robe once more and brushed his lips against Maddox's jaw.

"I'm...wonderful."

The celestial token on the nightstand glowed, the light almost pulsing, and Maddox stretched over Killian. As soon as he closed his fingers over the relic, he was ripped away from the witch and found himself standing naked in front of Azrael.

The archangel crossed his arms over his massive chest. His gaze roved up and down Mad's body.

"Maddox. What do you have to say for yourself?"

Oh, shit.

Azrael frowned. "That sort of language is not appreciated here."

Despite the archangel's warning, the words ran on repeat in Maddox's head, and he covered his cock with his hands, since he'd been half-hard pressed against his witch. "I am sorry, Azrael. There was a curse..."

"You've failed, Maddox. In every way. Losing the celestial sand, choosing to stay on earth past the time you were allotted, and...*that*." Azrael nodded to Maddox's cupped hands. "You are an angel of the celestial realm. We do not have sex with those who are of the earth."

"I'm half-human. So, clearly, *we* do," Maddox retorted. "My mother—"

"Your mother was banished for her actions, fell in love with a demon, and died for it."

Maddox took a step back as his eyes started to burn. He'd never known his mother or his father, only Sinclair. After his mother had died, the archangel Michael had brought Sin to the celestial realm, and the two brothers had been inseparable until Sin decided to try to find his father and had, instead, met La Fiura. "Send me back, Azrael."

"Why? So you can further these...*human* endeavors? The sand is gone. There is no reason for you to go back to earth." The archangel turned, but Maddox lunged for his arm. Azrael arched a brow and glared at Mad's fingers wrapped around his robes. "Choose your next words very carefully, Maddox."

Azrael's anger was a physical presence, almost as imposing as the archangel himself. Maddox scrambled for a legitimate reason to return to earth, stammering until Azrael yanked his arm free. Then it hit him.

"The witches believe Killian took the sand. They'll kill him for it. I have to fix this, Azrael. Otherwise, my soul will forever bear the stain of his death. Please. Let me return to the earthen realm to fix this."

Azrael frowned. "I cannot argue with your desire to make things right. However, if you do not return to the celestial realm in two earth days, the doorway will close, and you will live the rest of your life—however long that may be—on earth. You will keep your wings, and you will age slowly. But your body will eventually become mortal. Do not make this decision lightly, Maddox. If you stay on earth, you *will* die. And then...your soul will make the same trip as all the others. Whether you wish it to or not."

KILLIAN

Four hours. He'd paced and prayed for four hours, waiting for Maddox to return and hoping the whole time he wasn't gone for good. But he knew. Deep down, he knew Maddox had returned to the celestial realm without even saying goodbye.

The sheets still smelled like Maddox, like their coupling, and more than once, Killian found himself crushing the pillow to his chest. He'd been a bloody fool. Giving his heart to the angel, knowing Maddox would have to return to his own realm... But he'd thought, maybe...after what they'd shared, Mad would at least stick around for a day or two. Long enough for them to fuck one another in every manner possible.

Checking the time, Killian groaned. Almost five in the evening. If he were going to ring Beatrix, he needed to do it now.

"It's about bloody time," she said when the call

connected. "Some no-good git curses the lot of you at the ball and you wait almost a full day to call me? I thought you were smarter than that, Killian."

"In the past twenty hours, I've been cursed—which, by the way, destroyed my dampening cuff—rescued an angel after he stole celestial sand from the crypt under Magnolia House, been summoned, questioned, and locked in the coven's dungeon, hit by a spell the likes of which I'd prefer never to feel again, and have been branded with a pair of wings. Pardon me if I haven't been the most communicative bloke on the planet."

Magic sparked from his fingertips, and he groaned. "I need help, High Priestess. I can't control my magic without the cuff, and I feel like I'm about to come out of my skin."

Beatrix's voice gentled. "You won't, Killian Wade, because you know what happens when you lose control. But you are also too smart for your own good, I think."

"What are you on about?" Killian sank back down onto the bed and ran a hand through his hair. Fuck. He missed Maddox. Missed the angel's calming presence, his touch. His voice.

"You were born under a Blood Moon. That, combined with the specific *circumstances* of your birth mean your magic is the strongest of this age. But you were always frightened of it."

"And why should I not be? I killed a vampire, High Priestess. Oliver should have been much stronger than I could ever be. And one spell took his life."

"Magic does not exist in a vacuum, Killian. It depends on our emotions, our very life force, to exist and do its work. The man you thought you loved was about to die, and you tried to protect him. Had you done nothing, he would have died anyway."

"That doesn't change the fact that his last sight in this world was me, casting the spell that ended him."

Beatrix sighed. "No. It does not. But you are older and wiser now, witch. Ten years have passed, and you understand what you did wrong. We have been over this time and time again. If you tried the same spell today, it would not have the same effects."

"Bollocks. If I never cast a spell again, it will be too soon. I've had to use my magic twice since I got here, and each time...could have killed so many." Unable to sit still any longer, Killian dropped to his knees by the mini-bar and pulled out two tiny bottles of scotch.

Downing one after the other in a single swallow, he let the burn settle down his throat. His fingers traced the lines of the brand, and a powerful ache started deep in his core. "What do I do about this fecking curse?"

"Do you remember the words?"

"I won't repeat it all, but the punchline was this: *I damn you to your darkest fear. I bind you to dread's cold embrace. Until your truth you boldly face,*" Killian said.

Beatrix huffed out a wry laugh. "Fitting, I suppose. You must face your darkest fear. Overcome it. I am assuming you do not need me to tell you what that is."

Killian groaned. "I have to confront Jezebel. Use my magic. Willingly. And risk another's death."

"Yes. I cannot help you with this, Killian. It is something you must do alone. I do hope you will not destroy all of New Orleans while you are at it."

As do I, Killian thought as he ended the call. He was on his own.

～

MADDOX

Azrael returned him to the precise location he'd left from. The bed he'd shared with Killian. Except, it was empty.

Fuck. He'd been gone eight hours. Maddox knew time in the celestial realm went slower than that on earth. But he hadn't expected a ten-minute conversation to take eight earth hours. What had Killian thought? That he'd left? For good?

The clothing bags had been rifled through, and a sandwich wrapper lingered in the trash can. On the bedside table, Maddox found a note.

Maddox, I know what I have to do. Facing Jezebel is the only way to break my curse. Don't try to find me. If I live through the next few hours, I'll return. If not, I doubt I will ever see the celestial realm. Not after what I've done. The short time we had here, in this room...I will hold onto those memories. I wish we'd had more time. -Killian

"Shit, shit, shit." Maddox got dressed as quickly as he could, then ran downstairs, hoping to find Frank. The older gentleman sat at the front desk with a crossword puzzle in front of him.

"So there y'are," Frank said, a hint of judgement in his scratchy voice. "That man of yours brought down the sammich I got for you and said he wasn't sure if you were coming back. The two of you have a fight or something?"

"No." Maddox rubbed the back of his neck. "I...needed some air and got lost. I don't know this city. Did Killian say where he was going?"

"Nope. Just thanked me for dropping off the clothes and the sammich, said you wouldn't be needing this one, and that he hoped I had a good day." Frank set his pen down and leaned forward. "You going after him?"

"Yes. But I don't know where he went. I need to get to Bourbon Street. Can you point me in the right direction?"

"You'll need to get a cab, son." Frank reached for the telephone, but Maddox laid a hand on his wrist.

"I don't. Just...point me in the right direction." There was no way Maddox was going to wait for a cab. Not when he could fly across the city in minutes. Assuming Azrael hadn't taken away all of his powers.

Frank shrugged. "Out the door, head left. Bourbon Street is due east of here." He pointed behind him. "That way."

"Thank you, Frank. We'll be back." Maddox pushed through the door, keeping his voice low. "I hope."

TEN MINUTES LATER, he landed gently in an alley two blocks from Bourbon Street. He had to find the House of Voodoo and Sin's friend Mist. If he were going to help Killian, he needed backup.

The House of Voodoo, despite the name, was bright inside. Every single inch of free space on the walls was taken up by oddities. Everything from actual chicken bones to rubber masks of pig heads with long horns. Dozens of tourists whispered and pointed as they wove through the shop, and the man behind the counter explained the use of a small, strange-looking broom in cleansing rituals.

The sun had set less than half an hour ago. Would this Mist be here yet? Making his way to the back of the shop, Maddox pushed through a black, beaded curtain.

"Are you here for a reading?" The woman sounded young. No more than twenty-five, and as Maddox's eyes adjusted to the dim light, he took in her pale skin, the stillness to her limbs, and her amber eyes.

"That depends. Would you know where I can find Mist?" Keeping his gaze locked on the petite vampire, he reached out with his unique gifts so no one else coming in the room would see what he was about to do.

"I do not know that name," she said, but the hitch in her voice belied her words.

Maddox shrugged out of the leather jacket, then pulled his t-shirt over his head to unfurl his wings. "My brother, Sinclair, tells me Mist is always here after dark."

"Sin. Is he all right?" Mist was in front of him before Mad could blink, and her cool fingers gripped his upper arms. "The darkness is coming. Something so vile, it could destroy the entire world."

"Sin's fine. Out in San Francisco and working for a human-paranormal investigative firm." Maddox drew his wings back against his body, extricated himself from Mist's grip, and pulled his t-shirt back on before he gestured to the table Mist had been sitting at. "I need your help."

"Anything. Sin saved my life ten years ago. I would have met the sun without him." The vampire brushed her blond hair away from her face, revealing three long scars down her right cheek.

"What do you know about a witch named Jezebel?"

KILLIAN

He wouldn't go to Magnolia House. That would be suicide. Instead, he asked the cab driver to take him to Lafayette Cemetery No 1. This time of night, well after dark, the sacred burial grounds would be closed, and the only beings that he could hurt with his magic would be the ghosts. At least they couldn't die a second time.

Once he arrived, he pulled out the box of salt he'd picked up at a local convenience store a few blocks from the row house. Drawing a large circle in a patch of grass in the center of the grounds, Killian breathed deeply three times. Standing at the center, he closed his eyes. "I summon a circle of protection. May only love reside within."

With his right index finger, he pointed east. "I call the Air and the Guardian of the East to protect this sacred circle." Bowing to the air elemental he knew would be hiding in the mists, he then turned south. "May the element of Fire and the Guardian of the South protect this sacred circle." Water in the west and earth to the north followed, and when he finished drawing the perimeter, Killian turned his gaze to the sky. "May the Divine watch over this sacred space, fill it with love, peace, and protection."

A beam of light shone down upon him, spreading through his entire body, and sinking into the earth under his feet. The protective bubble carried the scent of his magic, and for the first time in a decade, it didn't smell like blood, fear, and burnt flesh. Instead, the scent of the sea, fresh and clean, surrounded him.

Holding out his left hand, Killian drummed the fingers of his right hand over his palm. "Light meets dark, wrong meets right. I will atone for all my sins this night. Find the witches I seek, call them to me, so this curse shall break and all be free."

A spark formed, growing steadily brighter, until it grew to the size of a marble. Picturing Jezebel and Delphine in his mind, he sent his charm to seek them out and bring them to him.

Killian sat in the center of the circle for an hour. Jezebel and Delphine obviously didn't care about punctuality. Or, he was a pitiful witch and couldn't cast a spell worth shite.

For what felt like the fiftieth time, he checked his phone. No messages. Nothing from Maddox, Jezebel, Delphine, or Beatrix. Though, it's not like Maddox had a phone of his own.

"Shut it," he muttered to himself. "He's gone. Back in the celestial realm where he belongs. He'll be safe there. And you...you'll move on. Someday."

"Killian Wade!" Jezebel shouted from beyond a row of gravestones to the east. The fog was so thick he couldn't see shite. "You will pay for your crimes!"

"Show yourself, Jeze. I have committed no crime save being young and reckless," Killian said as he pushed to his feet.

"And what about stealing the celestial sand?" This from Delphine, and Killian spun around to the west, where a heavy rain had started to fall, a curtain that shielded the High Priestess from view.

"Are the two of you proper cowards?" Killian called out. "Face me. Just outside the circle. Let us talk like civilized people."

The two witches approached, though Killian could see nothing but the rain and the mists. Still, he felt them. Their magic pulsed with every step, pressing in on him, almost crushing him.

The circle held, barely, and Killian struggled to breathe, to stand tall as the two most powerful witches in New Orleans stalked closer.

A spell bounced off the circle, sending sparks raining

down onto the wet grass. The salt would soon wash away, but the circle would remain as long as his own magic held.

"What happened to a proper discussion?" Killian asked as he clenched his fists, the magic sparking all along the tips of his fingers. "Jezebel, I was a sodding idiot when I was twenty-three, scared out of my mind, and half in love with your brother. I tried to save him."

"And yet you staked him and set his heart to flame. That isn't love, Killian." Jezebel started a low chant, and the ground under him started to rumble. A crack in the earth opened a few feet beyond the circle, widening slowly and heading right for him.

"You will pay for your crimes, witch," Delphine said from right behind him. Killian whirled around to find her flanked by a trio of her coven royalty and two of the burly guards who'd bound him in iron only this morning.

"I offer up only the truth." Killian stepped to the very edge of the circle. "You know of the blood oath, yes?"

"Of course." The rain slowed to a trickle as Delphine inclined her head, her black curls falling over one shoulder. "You willingly take the oath?"

"I will. If you call off your hell-cat."

Delphine snapped her fingers, and Jezebel swore under her breath. "You promised me revenge," she growled.

"And you will have it. After Killian takes the oath."

Jezebel took her place at Delphine's side and stared daggers at Killian. If she could kill him with looks alone, she'd do so, happily.

Killian pulled a small silver knife from his pocket and slid it across his palm. Blood welled, a deep crimson, and he made a fist, letting his life force drip onto the grass at his feet.

"I pledge my life, here and now. Let this be my final vow. If I lie, if truth I hide, may this circle fail and die."

Killian's entire body seized, and he strained against the spell. "Ask...me...anything," he managed.

Delphine pressed her hands against the circle, but it resisted her, to Killian's relief. "Did you steal the celestial sand from the crypt?"

"No." The answer flowed easily, truth the only option he had.

"Who did?"

Killian tried to protect Maddox, but the spell forced the words from his lips. "An...angel."

The *whoosh* of wings had to be all in his head. Maddox was back in the celestial realm. But then, he could see nothing but white feathers, a toned, muscular back, and dark, wavy hair.

"I stole the sand, witch. If you have a problem with that, you may deal with me, personally." Maddox's wings tucked against his back, and he tossed a quick glance over his shoulder. "I understand now, baby. What I need to do."

Mad stepped from the circle, and Killian's entire world went white.

CHAPTER TWELVE

MADDOX

H e'd thought flying was a fast way to travel. That was nothing compared to Mist carrying him halfway across the city in all of two minutes. By the time they reached the graveyard, Killian was surrounded by half a dozen witches, his hand bloody, and his body rigid.

Mist had warned him. "A blood oath. It compels him to utter only truths. Go to him. I will do what I can with the witches. *Without* killing them." She rolled her eyes, clearly unhappy with the promise Maddox had elicited from her before they'd set out.

Now, Maddox spread his wings, shielding Killian as he approached Delphine, Jezebel, and three other witches flanking them. "The sand didn't belong to you. I attempted to return it to its rightful place in the celestial realm."

"Attempted?" Delphine took a step closer, her eyes narrowing. "Where is the sand, angel?"

"Scattered to the four winds." He shrugged, his feathers rustling. "I suppose a few grains may have found ill humans to cure, but most were likely washed away by the afternoon rains. Killian had nothing to do with the theft. I broke into the crypt. Killian's only crime was rescuing me outside of Magnolia House with the broken vial in my pocket."

Delphine sidestepped Jezebel so she could see around Maddox to Killian. "Does the angel speak the truth, witch? Tell me where all of the grains went. Tell me everything."

Killian groaned and staggered under the weight of the spell. "I found him. Outside. The vial...was broken." Each word seemed to take more effort than the last, and Maddox turned and met Killian's gaze. Sorrow lingered in the blue-gray depths, and he whispered, "I'm sorry," before continuing. "Some of the sand fell...onto Maddox. The rest, I scattered."

"Onto the angel?" Delphine chuckled. "Well, then. They can be recovered."

"Maddox, get back into the circle!" Mist shouted, but at the same time, two large men leapt forward and grabbed Maddox by the arms. He struggled to free himself, but they were too strong, looping chains around his torso, binding his wings to his back and his arms at his sides.

"No. Delphine. Please," Killian begged, but the elder witch laughed, shoving her hands out in front of her and sending an arc of blue light into Mad's chest.

Agony overtook him. Burning, twisting, breaking bones and rending flesh. Blood dripped down his bare chest as the grains worked their way out of his body, and he screamed, thrashing within his chains.

All of his injuries from being hit by the car came back

with a vengeance, made worse by the chains and Azrael's warning in his ears. *"You will eventually become mortal."*

A percussive force slammed into him, and Maddox was launched high in the air, back over Killian's head, and when he came down, his body bowed over a tall grave marker. His spine shattered, and his legs went numb, but still, the grains fought their way free, and through his tunneled vision, he saw them float on the wind towards Delphine.

"Killian," he whispered. "Help...me..."

KILLIAN

No. He'd tried to bring Maddox back into the circle, but the spell had been too powerful, and now the angel lay bent over backwards, blood staining his lips, pouring from a dozen wounds in his chest, and still bound by those bloody chains.

"No more," he growled and stalked towards Delphine and Jezebel. "You are killing an angel. One of the Divine."

And the man I love.

He would not consign Maddox to Oliver's fate. Jeze charged him, but Killian held the memory of Maddox's touch, of his voice, his scent, and his kiss as he deflected Jezebel's magic, tossing her into a soft pile of dirt twenty feet away. She landed with a dull *oomph*, and Killian turned, using one hand to shield himself from Delphine's attack while the other loosened the chains from his angel and sent them wrapping around Jezebel.

The other witches were currently occupied fighting a pale, petite blond woman who moved so quickly, she could only be one thing—a vampire. With Jeze rendered temporarily unable to cast a spell, Killian turned to Delphine.

The words came to him, words he'd never learned but somehow knew would break the curse if he could just control his magic long enough to send the spell right where it needed to go.

"What is taken with vile intent will now be used to end torment. I face my truth, claim my rights, I will fear no more this night. Dread's cold embrace will let me be, that I may save my love from thee."

The crevasse just beyond his circle snapped closed, the tremor rolling through the ground all the way to Delphine. The High Priestess lost her footing and dropped to one knee, a bright ball of magical energy spinning in one palm, the vial half-full of celestial sand in the other.

Fear snaked icy fingers around his heart, but he had no choice. If he didn't release the spell gathering inside him, Maddox would die, and Killian...he might as well die then too. Already the angel's whimpers were so weak, he had to strain to hear them.

"I warned you, Delphine. What happens next...it is on you."

With his love for his angel burning brightly inside him, he let go, flinging his arms wide.

Purple and blue light swirled around him, faster and faster until he could see nothing but a tornado of colors. And then the eddy widened, spreading out in all directions. Jezebel screamed, and in front of him, Delphine disappeared into nothingness.

"Killian." The single, whispered word sent terror flooding him, and Killian raced over to Maddox, now lying on the ground next to the gravestone.

His bare chest was covered in blood, his left wing twisted, and his back still bent at an unnatural angle. "Mad, you're going to be okay," Killian said as he cupped the angel's cheeks and leaned down to kiss him.

"No. Too...far gone," Maddox choked out as tears streaked down his temples. "Even the sand...can't help me now."

"No, but I can." The vampire knelt on Maddox's other side, bared her fangs, and slashed at her wrist. She held it close to his lips. "Drink, angel. This will hurt. Worse than anything you've ever imagined. But it will keep you alive until your body heals on its own."

Maddox shuddered as the first drop of vampire blood spilled onto his lips. "Love you," he mouthed, then his eyes fluttered closed.

"No! Do something, vampire!" Killian said as he took Maddox's hand and held it to his lips.

The woman arched a brow and shoved her bleeding wrist harder against Maddox's mouth. "What do you think I'm trying to do, witch? If he's dead, I can't *force* the blood down his throat."

"He's not dead. He's not." Killian rested one hand over Maddox's heart and the other on the vamp's shoulder. *"Mark this place and stop this time."*

A subtle warmth infused him, and as Killian cast his gaze around the cemetery. the blades of grass were perfectly still, droplets of rain hovered in the air, but at his side, the vampire swore softly. "Drink, angel. By the ancient gods, *drink.*"

Killian pressed his lips to Maddox's temple. "Please, angel. *My* angel. Come back to me."

The woman pulled her wrist away and licked the wound. It healed before Killian's eyes. "Vampire—?"

Maddox sputtered and coughed, then curled onto his side towards Killian. "Fuck, that...hurts, Mist."

"I told you." Mist patted his shoulder. "Release the spell, witch. And tell me what to do with the one you called Jezebel. She is the only one still conscious."

Killian looked from the vampire to his angel. "Leave her. Let her spend the night here to think about what she's done. Mad?"

With a groan, Maddox wrapped an arm around Killian's waist and tried to raise himself up, and Killian fell back on his arse and pulled Maddox against him.

"You're a bloody fool," Killian said sharply. "Don't risk yourself for me again."

"Had a whole plan. Didn't know she could pull the sand back...out of me." Maddox shifted his legs, then sighed. "Thought I was a goner."

"You almost were." Killian cupped the back of Maddox's neck and kissed him. "You taste of vampire blood. We are going to have to fix that."

"What did you have in mind?" Stronger now, Maddox almost managed to get to his knees, then scanned the cemetery. "Fuck, Killian. What did you do?"

"I saved you. And broke the curse. The rest...I think the rest needs whiskey."

CHAPTER THIRTEEN

KILLIAN

The vampire, Mist, spat on Jezebel before vanishing into the night muttering something about finding her sisters before the entire world went to Hell. Maddox let Killian wrap an arm around his waist as they made their way out of the cemetery.

As soon as they were outside the gates, Killian stopped and looked down at his angel. "I can get us somewhere...safe —if you trust my magic."

"I always trusted your magic," Mad said with a weak smile. "Do you?"

"Now, yeah. I do." Guiding Maddox's arms around his neck, Killian held his love's gaze as he whispered the spell that carried them across the ocean, back to the English countryside, where they reappeared in Killian's bedroom at sunrise.

It had felt so...*right* to protect his angel, to have Maddox in his arms. He wanted this one day. He couldn't think about what would happen when Maddox went back to the celestial realm for good.

"Where are we?" Maddox asked as he trailed his fingers over the duvet.

"My home." Killian tugged Maddox's hand and led him into the bath. Though he'd never admitted it to anyone, the bathtub was his favorite part of this house. Stripping his angel of the bloodstained pants and briefs as the tub filled, Killian couldn't find the words he so desperately wanted to say.

Maddox sank into the hot water with a groan, and though Killian ached to join him, Mad looked like he'd been run over by a train. Now was *not* the time to indulge his dick, even though it strained against his trousers.

"I'll make us a pot of tea," Killian said as he pressed a kiss to the top of Maddox's head.

"Uh huh." The angel was half asleep, his head resting on the back of the tub, arms draped over the sides. He'd hidden his wings, and as Killian headed for the stove, he wondered just how that worked.

Tiny padded into the room as Killian arranged mugs, a bowl of sugar, and a small pitcher of milk on a tray. "So, you survived," the cat said and yawned.

"No thanks to you." With a flick of his wrist, Killian summoned the milk from the cold box and poured some into a bowl for Tiny.

"Magic?" His familiar crept closer to the bowl, as if she were convinced the milk had to be poison. "This is new."

"Found a spot of clarity in New Orleans." Another spell shut the back door, and Killian arched a brow. "Perhaps now, you'll consider being a proper familiar."

Tiny sat and cocked her head. "Perhaps. Summon me a plate of tuna and we'll talk."

"Done." The spell flowed easily, and Tiny jumped back as a plate with the flaky fish appeared in front of her. "Things are going to change around here."

"About damn time." Tiny sniffed at the tuna, then dove in with abandon, pausing only to peer up at Killian with narrowed eyes. "Is the angel staying?"

Killian almost dropped the teapot. "The angel?"

"The one in your bathtub? Really, Killian...I didn't think you were that daft."

"I'm not. But how did you know?" He poured the hot water over the teabags, breathing deeply as the rich scent wafted over him.

"I'm a familiar, not an idiot. His energy is unmistakable. Is he staying? I'll alter the wards on the house."

"I don't...know."

"How can you say that?" Maddox asked from the bedroom doorway. A towel hung low around his hips, and though his chest was scarred from the sand trying to escape, his bruises were almost gone now, leaving only dusky skin and all those muscles. "Killian, I love you."

Killian swallowed hard, the lump of emotion in his throat suddenly threatening to choke him. Striding over to his angel, he wrapped his arms around Maddox, holding on so tightly, he could feel Mad's heartbeat. "I have never felt for anyone what I feel for you. I love you, Maddox. My angel. You saved me. In so many ways."

"You saved me too." Drawing back slightly, Maddox kissed him, their tongues dancing in a war for dominance that Killian would *not* let Maddox win. Not now. For now, he wanted his angel on his back, in bed, screaming his name.

THANK you for reading Wicked Omens. I love Mad and Killian, and you can see them again in *Storm of Sin*. One-click **STORM OF SIN** now. For an exclusive excerpt, just turn the page!

SNEAK PEEK - STORM OF SIN

SINCLAIR

Commander Jones slammed his hand down on the desk. "Stop with the excuses. I warned you there would be consequences for your actions. Now get out of my sight. Your new partner arrives in a few hours. Maybe you want to take care of your little...problem before that happens?"

Fuck.

Sinclair shoved the commander's door with as much force as he could muster given the hunger currently eating away at me. Damn earthquake. Barely even a three-point-five, but enough to cause everyone at the Midnight Coven—his favorite feeding grounds—to evacuate before he'd settled on a snack for the evening.

He caught sight of his reflection in the two-way glass outside Interrogation Room Three, and cursed again. He was normal enough looking after he'd fed. Now, his stomach empty, he resembled a cross between George Clooney, Jason Momoa, and Channing Tatum. Bursting out of headquarters, he turned half a dozen heads—mostly women, but the occasional man as well—and three of them headed straight for him.

"Are you a movie star?" The meek little mouse in front of him didn't have enough power in her for a snack, let alone a full meal. But maybe she could take the edge off.

"No," Sin purred as he took her arm. "But I've often thought I should be. What role would you like me to play?" They headed for an alley, and she prattled on about how he'd make a great vampire or werewolf.

"Or you could star in one of those BDSM movies...you know...the ones that are all over right now. Anything, really."

"What's your name, love?" One rule. He had to know a woman's name before he stole a bit of her life force. Well, two rules. No killing. He might be a demon, but he wasn't a monster.

She gazed up at him with wide brown eyes. "L-Laura Hallstrop."

"Nice to meet you, Laura Hallstrop," he said as he scanned the alley for witnesses. Good. Not even a drunk sleeping things off. Choosing the cleanest section of wall he could, he caged Laura Williams with his forearms pressed to the bricks. "May I kiss you?"

"Y-yes," she stammered, and he crushed his lips to hers. Fuck. So sweet. And stronger than he'd thought. Her life force flowed as he danced his tongue with hers, and the little nip to her lower lip elicited a moan. From him.

Laura melted against the bricks, and soon, he had to wrap his arms around her slight frame to hold her upright. She clawed at his shirt, desperate for more, but as he probed her mind, he saw a husband, two kids. Fuck. Breaking off the kiss, he cupped her cheek, his other arm still tight around her back. "Look at me, Laura."

She gasped. Unsurprising. With the power coursing through him and the feeding haze at its peak, his normally dark blue eyes were probably blood red. His voice took on a low, soothing tone "Where were you going when you saw me?"

"The bank." Enraptured, she gave him a lazy smile. "We could go to a hotel."

"No, sweetheart. Now pay attention." With another brief kiss, he locked his mind on hers. "You headed to the bank, but then you heard a kitten crying down this alley. You took a detour to see if you could find it, but once you reached the alley, the sound stopped. You looked around for a few minutes, but never found the poor little thing, so you returned to your errands."

He broke their connection and stepped back, using a bit of his newly refreshed power to hide himself with a bit of glamour. Laura shook her head and rubbed the back of her neck. "Here kitty, kitty. Are you still here?"

After another minute, she shrugged, straightened her jacket, and almost floated out of the alley. She'd remember nothing, other than how amazing she felt. Dropping the glamour, Sin headed in the opposite direction in search of another willing victim.

ONE-CLICK Storm of Sin now!

About the Author

Patricia D. Eddy writes romance for the beautifully broken. Fueled by coffee, wine, and Doctor Who episodes on repeat, she brings damaged heroes and heroines together to find their happy ever afters in many different worlds. From military to paranormal to BDSM, her characters are unstoppable forces colliding with such heat, sparks always fly.

Patricia makes her home in Seattle with her husband and very spoiled cats, and when she's not writing, she loves working on home improvement projects, especially if they involve power tools.

Her award-winning *Away From Keyboard* series will always be her first love, because that's where she realized the characters in her head were telling their own stories—and she was just writing them down.

You can reach Patricia all over the web...
patriciadeddy.com
patricia@patriciadeddy.com

facebook.com/patriciadeddyauthor
twitter.com/patriciadeddy
instagram.com/patriciadeddy
bookbub.com/profile/patricia-d-eddy

ALSO BY PATRICIA D. EDDY

AWAY FROM KEYBOARD

Dive into a steamy mix of geekery and military prowess with the men and women of Hidden Agenda and Second Sight.

Breaking His Code

In Her Sights

On His Six

Second Sight

By Lethal Force

Fighting For Valor

Finding Their Forevers (a holiday short story)

Call Sign: Redemption

Braving His Past

Protecting His Target

Defending His Hope

Trusting His Instincts

GONE ROGUE (AN AWAY FROM KEYBOARD SPINOFF SERIES)

Rogue Protector

Rogue Officer

Rogue Survivor

Rogue Defender

DARK PNR

These novellas will take you into the darker side of the paranormal
with vampires, witches, angels, demons, and more.

Forever Kept

Immortal Hunter

Wicked Omens

Twisted Captive

Storm of Sin

BY THE FATES

Check out the COMPLETE By the Fates series if you love dark and
steamy tales of witches, devils, and an epic battle between good
and evil.

By the Fates, Freed

Destined: A By the Fates Story

By the Fates, Fought

By the Fates, Fulfilled

IN BLOOD

If you love hot Italian vampires and and a human who can hold her own against beings far stronger, then the In Blood series is for you.

Secrets in Blood

Revelations in Blood

HOLIDAYS AND HEROES

Beauty isn't only skin deep and not all scars heal. Come swoon over sexy vets and the men and women who love them.

Mistletoe and Mochas

Love and Libations

RESTRAINED

Do you like to be tied up? Or read about characters who do? Enjoy a fresh COMPLETE BDSM series that will leave you begging for more.

In His Silks

Christmas Silks

All Tied Up For New Year's

In His Collar